NORTH

BILLIONAIRE RANCH
BOOK 1

VANESSA VALE

North by Vanessa Vale

Cover design: Bridger Media

Cover graphic: Deposit Photos: designwest

1

JED

I DIDN'T FUCK on command.

I hated being told what to do, even by my boss at the FBI. Go undercover, she'd ordered, in the small corner of Montana where you grew up because no one else could blend in as a cowboy. I sure as hell didn't blend in as a suit and tie G-Man. But that meant I had to settle into my old community not as the star football quarterback they all remembered but in the false persona of a disgraced FBI agent returning to the homestead.

If that wasn't enough, being ordered around by the men I was trying to bring down was a pain in my fucking ass. I gritted my teeth and did what they wanted although quitting and being a *real* disgraced FBI agent was looking better and better.

Because I'd never expected to be told what to do with my dick.

If I was twenty again, I'd have been thrilled with the assignment. Easy pussy.

Now? I was questioning my entire career because it led me to this.

To a wake at Billionaire Ranch. No one around here called it anything but that because the nickname explained it all.

I parked in the field along with everyone else who'd come during calling hours, then hoofed it to the big house. House? Nah. It was a fucking mansion. Log walls and huge windows. River rock and slate roof. No doubt the driveway I walked up was heated to keep off the heavy snow.

The massive front doors were open with people spilling out onto the wide porch and front lawn. They were either dressed in black or in crisp jeans and shirts, the closest thing to mourning-wear for Montanans.

I tipped my hat to a woman who offered me a small smile, as if she was offering me comfort at this difficult time.

She didn't know I wasn't here to offer my condolences, but to fuck some answers out of the newly crowned queen of the Wainright family.

North. Fucking. Wainright.

It'd been over ten years since I'd laid eyes on her. At seventeen, she'd been my baby brother's girlfriend. And jailbait. I'd been the twenty-seven-year-old who'd come home to visit for the Fourth of July weekend and saw her at a family picnic.

I'd kept the fact that I'd thought her gorgeous to myself. Hell, every man who'd ever laid eyes on her would agree with me. She'd been so fucking pretty in a white sundress, her blonde hair long down her back. I hadn't talked to her. Not once, staying as far away from someone who was too tempting and too illegal. I'd had no intention of poaching my brother's girl or robbing the cradle for a date. But she'd been... memorable and that made her dangerous.

I'd headed back to DC and she'd dumped Jock a few weeks later. She hadn't crossed my mind since. Until now. My job was to connect Macon Wainright to corruption, which meant me being a lackey for John Marshall, because Marshall had been *his* lackey.

To everyone around here, I was now only a bored cowboy with dangerous tendencies.

Marshall had been more than eager to hire me. I

wasn't sure if his middle name was Corrupt or Unethical.

When Wainright died five days ago, he and Marshall had been in the middle of a deal. Marshall had millions to lose so now he had a hard-on to get North Wainright. To ensure the deal would go through. He figured the best way for an ice princess like her to talk was to thaw her out with a big dick and bigger orgasms.

My cell vibrated and I pulled it from my pocket as I stepped into the foyer. "Barnett," I murmured.

People looked my way, but didn't pay me any mind, returning to their muted conversations. One woman blotted her eyes with a tissue, the only obvious mourner I could see.

"Well?"

I knew the voice. Marshall was a persistent fuck.

"Macon Wainright's definitely dead." That was the only thing I knew for certain. He was lying in a casket ten feet away in a snap shirt and bolo tie, hands folded across his chest. His usually tan complexion was waxy. It seemed the only time I wouldn't see a sneer on his face was when he'd been pumped full of embalming fluid.

I was sure I wasn't the only one thinking that.

"That's all you've got for me?"

I was too old to kowtow to the asshole. I wasn't a *yes* man. Never had been. I might be doing his bidding. I might be doing it so I could see his ass in prison, but I wasn't going to make his life easier beforehand.

My attention was snagged on a woman coming down the stairs, a yellow lab following right behind. The place was so fucking fancy it had two stairwells, left and right, that turned and met in the middle. In this case, Macon Wainright in all his dead glory was what was centered instead of perhaps a table with a vase of fresh flowers.

North Wainright. She sure as shit wasn't seventeen any longer. I remembered the long, blonde hair. The high cheekbones. Full lips. Blue eyes.

But the grown version of North Wainright in the flesh and a black dress that hugged her lush womanly curves... not to mention fuck me stilettos that did exceptional things for her legs—

Fuck me.

Right. I was supposed to do just that. Get her to fuck me.

If one of her brothers had inherited the CEO position of Wainright Holdings at Macon's death, I doubted Marshall would expect me to fuck one of them for information. I didn't swing that way. But since Marshall was a sexist fuck, he figured the only way he'd get what he wanted from a woman was if she'd been well satisfied by some D.

My staring made me miss half of what Marshall was saying. "...need to know if she's keeping the deal."

"I know," I replied. "I'm here. I see her."

I hung up, shoved my cell back in my pocket. The guy wanted a job done. I'd do it, but I wasn't going to give him a play-by-play.

She approached her brother, nodded to him. Didn't smile. Didn't offer him a hug or a pat on the shoulder. She didn't hold a tissue in her elegant hand. Her eyes weren't red from crying.

East—yeah, they all had fucked up compass names—leaned toward her, whispered something in her ear. He was two years younger and looked nothing like her. Dark hair but ridiculously pale eyes. He was big and built like a fucking tank.

She glanced at the casket. Nodded in reply to whatever he said.

When I'd first gone undercover with Marshall, I'd learned the family's stats. While I was going to bring down Marshall, he was collateral. My prime target was Macon Wainright.

Except now he was dead. Massive heart attack while fucking his mistress. I glanced once again at the body, then turned away. The case on him would close along with the lid on his casket.

Since a dead guy couldn't go to jail, the prime target with the FBI now was North Wainright. She was thirty. Oldest of four kids to Macon Wainright and Kitty Southforth Wainright. Kitty'd been dead for twenty-five years. Macon for five days. Undergrad at Harvard. MBA from Wharton. Second-in-command at Wainright Holdings.

Well, in command now and had all the answers.

When a minister, reverend or whatever hell the guy's religious title was, sidled up to them and set his hand at North's elbow and she shifted away, I practically growled.

My gaze narrowed. The man of God was touching her. The action was impersonal, but I didn't fucking care. She was one gorgeous woman and I wanted to be the one to put my hands on her. She might have been innocent when she was seventeen, but she'd gotten dirty since then, I was sure. I was hard at the thought of being the one to get her dirty now. Of mussing her up. Of getting that lipstick smeared and all over my dick.

I felt my cell vibrate, knew it was Marshall again. He didn't like to be ignored. But that brought me back to reality. To why I was here for the wake.

It wasn't to pay my respects. I was here to fuck North Wainright. For Marshall. For stupid-ass pillow talk.

As my dick hardened down my thigh, I knew one thing was for certain. I was going to get her beneath me. I had a new mission now. To fuck her. Not for Marshall or the FBI.

For me.

Hell, for *her*.

Because once she discovered how I could get her off, she wouldn't go elsewhere.

Because now that I'd seen her again, no other woman was going to do. Fate? Love at first sight? Serendipity? I didn't give a shit. All I knew was this woman was mine.

East ditched her with the minister, which made me hate the kid. Brothers, even younger ones, should watch out for their sisters. The minister was speaking, clearly droning on about something. She didn't smile at him but offered the guy her full attention. At least that was what it looked like. I could tell—how, I had no fucking clue—she was elsewhere in her mind. Her ice castle where she escaped, perhaps.

I strode toward her, the timing perfect. A quick glance at Macon Wainright in the casket and maybe I was stretching it a bit, but I wasn't turning back now.

The wake was the only time the mansion's front door was flung open to the town. The burial would be later, but that was family only. I couldn't knock on the door and proposition her.

No, it was now or... sometime when it'd be a hell of a lot harder.

"There you are, princess," I said, sidling up beside North so our shoulders brushed. She wasn't a short woman and in those heels, she only had to glance up a few inches to meet my gaze. I took off my hat. "I've been looking for you."

North's pale brow arched and recognition flared in her eyes. Interesting. She remembered me.

I turned to the minister. "I hope you don't mind, Reverend, but North's needed in the study."

I didn't know where the hell the study was, or if this house had one, but it was big and fancy enough for the possibility.

The older man offered a kindly smile, one he'd probably practiced for decades to pull out at shindigs like this one.

I took North's elbow and steered her away from the man, turning to the right and into a huge living room. Animal heads lined the walls and a huge ten or twelve point elk hung over a cold fireplace. I veered around the guests and into the connecting room. Another sitting room. How many did this place have? I saw an open door and led her through, then shut it behind me, only after the dog followed, then dropped down on the rug and promptly went to sleep. We were in an office with a huge desk. Smaller animal heads lined one wall, antique and vintage guns lined the other.

"Jesus, what is this place?" I asked, taking in the carnage.

"My father's sanctuary," she stated, crossing her arms over her chest. The neckline of her dress wasn't flashy, but the motion pushed up her tits and I couldn't miss the soft swells.

I blinked, then looked away. "You planning on mounting him too?" I asked.

Her eyes widened at the suggestion, then she laughed. Her head tipped back and I couldn't miss the long column of her neck.

She was so fucking pretty.

"I thought about it over the years, but now's the time, isn't it? He'll be in the ground in a few hours."

Her voice was deep and husky. Sexy and surprising.

"Say the word, princess, and I'll have it done."

She cocked her head to the side, studied me. "I remember you."

"I remember you, too."

The smile slipped. "Jock's older brother."

"That's right. Jed Barnett. You and Jock have a history." She'd dated my brother. Probably gave him her V-card. Then dumped him, which had made her daddy dump a deal to buy my parents' land.

She glanced away but didn't look remorseful. She looked... icy. "That was a long time ago. Heard he's married with two kids now."

"Three," I corrected. I might be over ten years older than Jock, but he was the one who'd found someone and settled down. "Had a baby girl in April."

"I'm glad he found the woman he was supposed to love."

I frowned at her answer. I was expecting something a little more aloof. Calculating.

"What is it you want?" she asked.

"What makes you think I want something?"

"You lied to a minister and got me in here, Jed Barnett." She lifted her hand to indicate a room alone together.

"The whole town's here. Half are to see the inside of this place." I glanced around at the over-the-top office. "Half are here to see your daddy in a casket."

"Which one are you?" she asked, cocking her head to the side.

"Neither."

Based on the wide-eyed stare, the answer surprised her. "Then what are you here for?"

"You." My answer was simple. I didn't need to say more. It was the truth since I was doing Marshall's bidding. I could tell him about this private meeting. Keep him satisfied for a stretch.

As for fucking her?

As I'd said, I didn't fuck on command.

I wanted to satisfy North but doing that was only for me. I didn't usually get so hot for a woman. Sure, I'd picked up women. What forty-year-old hadn't? But this was different.

This was North Wainright. She was going to be a challenge.

Or was she? I couldn't miss the way her pupils dilated. Oh yeah, she liked that answer, but she wasn't going to let it show. I didn't want to play poker with this one.

"Seriously?"

I looked her over. "Dead serious."

"You've had thirteen years to make a move," she countered. "Why now? Why at my father's wake?"

I leaned against the door so she couldn't escape, unless she climbed out the big window in that dress and heels. "Would you have let me onto the property?"

She studied me. "I don't know. Are you dangerous?"

"To your panties."

A laugh accompanied an eye roll. "That work with other women?"

I shrugged. I might be undercover and be wrapped up in so many fucking lies, but I was going to be straight with her. She was too smart for anything else.

"I'm not interested in other women's panties. I'm interested in yours. In my pocket."

She turned and looked around the room. "You want to get it on in here? Not the most" —she slid her hand along the back of a tufted leather couch— "comfortable of places."

"You'd like it if I bent you over the arm of that sofa." I pointed. "That desk's exactly the right height to lay you on and eat you out. I'd say I could fuck you up against the wall, but it might be a little crowded with a dead deer on one side and a moose on the other."

Her mouth parted and her breath came in little pants.

"I'm to lift my dress and let you have your way just because you talk dirty?"

I shrugged, taking in the garment that probably cost more than my truck. "Only stating facts."

"Again, why now? I'd think you wouldn't want your

younger brother's sloppy seconds. Isn't that what guys say?"

My jaw clenched. The idea of Jock, or any guy, getting his dick in her had me seeing red. All I could think of was *mine.*

"Your daddy's laying in a casket out in the foyer. I haven't seen your other brothers, but East didn't seem like the consoling type. Figured you might need a shoulder to cry on."

She laughed again, although she wasn't all that amused. "Why should he console me when I have no reason to cry about my father dying? Besides, eating me out is a lot different than offering a shoulder."

She was blunt. I liked it. I'd think about why she wasn't mourning her father later.

"Whatever you need, princess," I offered.

Her eyes narrowed and she studied me. I remained still as she raked her gaze over me, from the tips of my buffed work boots to my dark hair.

"Anyone else ask you what you needed?" I doubted it. She had that cool control thing going for her. Untouchable.

She didn't respond, but the way her shoulders rolled back, I knew the answer was no. Interesting. She was a princess, but she was in a high tower all alone.

"Typical. A guy thinks a woman could only feel

better if she gets laid. You want to what... soften me up with a few orgasms?"

Exactly that.

"The only woman who'd question that is one who doesn't get laid very much," I countered.

A flush rose up from the neckline of her dress and traveled up to her cheeks. She spun away.

"What do you really want, Jed?" she asked as I admired her perfect ass. "Money? An *in* with one of my partners? A job?"

It was my turn to bristle. I wasn't sure if my down-on-my-luck cover was paying off and she thought I needed something to pay my bills, or she'd been hit up before. "I told you."

She spun back and wondered how she didn't tip over in those heels. Women in Montana didn't often sport business wear and stilts. The state was casual about everything. But the look did it for me. I wanted to get my hands on her and knock some of that shine off her business veneer.

"You came to the wake to pay your respects. You saw me, your dick got hard, and you want to do something about it. No guy comes on this strong."

"You're right. I saw you. My dick is definitely hard." Her gaze dropped to the front of my pants and her eyes flared wide. Yeah, I was big. It pleased me to know she was impressed. "I want you. Want to watch you come screaming my name."

She frowned, eyed me as if I'd come from another planet, one where men didn't only think of themselves. "You want to get *me* off."

It was my turn to narrow my eyes. "Princess, you say that as if no guy's ever put you first. I'm not sure if I should beat the shit out of them or thank them."

"I get off." She said that, then bit her lip as if the words slipped out. It seemed North didn't like to give any piece of herself away, even the smallest sliver of truth.

"With a man?"

She shrugged a slim shoulder. Sniffed and looked down her nose at me, even though I was inches taller. "Who needs one when batteries and high-grade silicone can do the job?"

I shook my head, pushed off the door. "Now that's a crying shame. A princess like you should be riding dick whenever she's running hot."

She wasn't appalled by my words. She hadn't smacked me. I'd call it a win... so far.

"And you're here to be that dick?"

"You're impressed by mine and you've only seen it in my jeans."

She paused, closed her eyes and slowly shook her

head. "This is insane. There are probably two hundred emails in my inbox waiting for a reply. My assistant is around here somewhere, hovering and waiting to update me on all the ways things are falling apart at the office since I've barely been in since I got the news about Macon. On top of that, I have a house full of people and a dead body in the other room."

Dead *body,* not dead *father.*

I shook my head at her, as if her excuses were petty. I could only imagine the shit she accomplished in a day. In high heels. I stepped close, stroked her cheek. Watched the way her blue eyes went dark. Her skin was like silk beneath my knuckles. My thumb brushed over her lower lip, back and forth. Then, when she didn't knee me in the balls, I lowered my head and kissed her. Watched her face until the last second when her lids fell closed. For a second she was stiff, then she melted like wax in the hot sun. She tasted like sunshine and sweetness, completely opposite of the image she intentionally offered to the world.

I didn't linger even though she kissed like a fucking dream.

"You're North Wainright," I murmured. "You want my dick, you want it now, make it happen. You remember me and by the way your nipples are poking against your dress, you liked what you saw then and what you see now. You don't need an assistant to pencil this into your planner."

She blinked, as if coming out of a trance.

Then she studied me for a minute, her shrewd, blue-eyed gaze raking over every inch of me once again in my jeans and snap shirt, my Stetson in my hand.

Turning, she went to the wall of guns, grabbed a shotgun off the lower mounts. I stepped back, raised my hands in front of me.

Shit, I'd gone about this fucking wrong. I liked my balls attached and it seemed she intended to remove them with a twelve gauge.

But she didn't even look my way. She opened it to see if there were shells, then snapped it shut, handling it like she knew what she was doing. Walking past me, she flung open the door and marched out of the room. I followed right on her heels, guests clearing a path for her.

She went over to her daddy's casket, raised her arm and knocked the lid down with a resounding crack, then went through the open front doors.

Standing on the porch, she raised the shotgun like she was a skeet shooting champion and fired into the air. The boom shook the crystal in the chandelier over my head. There were a few screams, many gasps and some panic.

"Wake's over," she called. "Everyone out."

People scurried out of her house like rats being caught in a spotlight. No one questioned a woman wielding a shotgun at her daddy's wake.

Hell, no one questioned North Wainright.

She turned and looked over her shoulder, her gaze meeting mine as guests streamed past. "Except you."

2

NORTH

"NORTH, DEAR. WHAT ABOUT THE FUNERAL?"

The minister must have felt good about his soul going to heaven because he didn't leave with all the other townsfolk. As Jed had pointed out, they'd eaten my food and drank my liquor just to see the inside of the house. No doubt my bold action with my still-warm shotgun would make the rounds in town within the hour.

No one gave a shit about my father because he hadn't cared about anyone but himself. Including me. I wasn't sad he was dead. Far from it. I hated the man.

Having Jed Barnett here was a reminder of that. Of

what Macon had done when I was seventeen. How he'd used me. He'd said he'd wanted to wait to finally put a kid to work for the company until I was eighteen, to bring me into his world, but the moment had been too good to pass up.

I took a deep breath, hoping the headache at the base of my skull would stop throbbing.

The minister was waiting for me to respond. He had to be sweating in the all-black outfit and tight white collar. Yet he seemed completely unruffled, as if firing shotguns at a wake happened every day. He was more concerned about getting the deceased buried.

I wanted my father's body out of the house and six feet under just as much. Probably more.

"Three o'clock as planned," I reassured him. This was one thing on my calendar I wasn't going to forget.

I shifted the shotgun to my other arm, the barrel aimed at the floor. My shoulder was a little sore from the kick, but at least I felt it. Felt *something.*

Besides exhaustion. Stress. Anger. I'd been bitter for so long, I forgot what sweet felt like. My lips still tingled with it.

Glancing over his shoulder, the minister gave the closed casket a peek, as if Macon might push the top back up and be angry because his wake had ended early.

"What the fu—heck was that?" East shouted, coming down the hall from the kitchen at the back of the house. He took one look at the minister and gave a contrite smile. "Sorry, Father."

"It was time for the party to end," I told him.

East looked out the open doorway to the slow stream of cars going down the drive.

"I should've thought of that," he grumbled, then shrugged. "Want a sandwich?"

I shook my head, eyeing the huge sub he had in his hand. There was a table covered with finger foods in the other room. A sandwich was the last thing I wanted. How anyone could eat with a dead body on display was beyond me.

This was all part of the will. Macon, being the center of attention one last time. I wasn't sure if the lawyers were going to bother me for cutting it short.

"You should relax, dear," the minister advised. "It's a difficult time. See you at three."

I gave him a nod and ushered him to the open doors, closing them behind him.

"Yeah, sis," East agreed, patting me on the shoulder as he turned and headed back toward the kitchen. "You should relax. Not that you know how."

I frowned. I'd been running a billion-dollar company with Macon, not like him grading papers as a university professor. He lived in Bozeman, rarely coming back to the ranch, even when he had his summers free. I didn't blame him. I wished I was him and had his carefree lifestyle. But I'd been groomed to carry on the name. To run the business.

He had no idea. No clue as to what I'd had to deal with. What I'd lived through. *Agreed to.* Survived. I'd sheltered him and my two other brothers, gave them the freedom to be what they wanted. I couldn't relax, because when I did, I didn't like what happened.

I caught Jed's eye as East disappeared toward the kitchen.

"Even the minister said to relax," Jed said finally. "Orgasms sanctioned by God." He came over to me with that long-legged swagger. "Even you can't argue with that," he added.

I rolled my eyes as I moved around him, leaving him to follow me. Or not.

He did, of course, back to the library. I'd have thought less of him if he'd given up now. I put the shotgun back on the mounts, then moved to my father's desk, leaned against it as Jed closed the door behind him.

God, I was as attracted to him as I was at seventeen. For the first time, I'd felt the stirrings of desire. Sure, I'd kissed his brother Jock, my boyfriend senior year of high school, fooled around a little, but he hadn't made me come alive as I had just by looking at twenty-seven-year-old Jed.

He was older now, around forty. His hair was almost black, but as he came closer, I could see threads of silver at the temples. The square jaw I'd thought could sharpen knives was now covered in a trimmed beard.

Over six feet of perfect body. His jeans molded to his thick thighs. His forearms were corded and tanned, sprinkled with dark hair. He was fit, as if he tossed hay bales or ran marathons. Or both.

I hated that men got better with age, while women got old. But Jed had, and in his case, I didn't mind. Maybe it was because I was looking at him through something other than a teenager's eyes. I saw him now in a completely different way. I wasn't expecting rainbows and fairy tales or love any longer. Only the emotionless release a hot guy wanted to give me. And he was hot. Then back to my regularly scheduled life.

The day Jock pointed out his older brother at their family barbecue was one of the last days I'd been naïve. I'd grown up that holiday weekend after learning Macon's plans to use me as part of a business deal. I started to build that protective wall of aloofness that I'd been adding bricks to ever since. I might lift my skirt, but I wasn't dropping any of my shields for a man.

I didn't know any other way. Macon had been dead for five days. Things hadn't changed at the office yet, but they would when I returned. I was CEO now and there was nothing my father could do to me any longer. I already had shares in the company and the will had only divided up his portion between his kids, although I'd been given majority interest. South, East, and West wanted nothing to do with it.

I could finally steer the company the way I wanted, the way my mother had wanted. The way it should have been since it was her family money that had started it.

Macon had been only the hired hand who'd charmed himself into her panties long enough to make me. Trap her into a loveless marriage where they somehow had sex two more times to make my brothers, one of those fun occasions making twins. Or maybe they weren't actually his, as I suspected.

"You're in your head, princess."

Jed stirred me from my thoughts. It was ironic he was the one offering himself. His services. I'd thought of him often when I was alone. Had the picture of the younger version of him in my head. When I had to think of something untouched, untainted by Macon.

To dream about. And now he was here.

Back then I'd been too young for him, of course. Why would Jed have wanted a seventeen-year-old girl? Or even notice one who'd been dating his little brother? He hadn't. In fact, I hadn't laid eyes on him since then. Until now.

Now. I sighed as I took in every inch of him. Even though he'd been a grown man all those years ago, he'd filled out since. He was thicker. More muscular. More intense. Focused. The white snap shirt fit him like a glove and God… even his hands were hot.

I hadn't been wrong back then about how hot he was, and he was even more so now. And instead of not seeing me like I'd thought all those years ago, he saw me now.

His whiskey-colored gaze was searching. Roving. Dark. As if life had tossed shit in his way and he'd dealt with it. Survived. I wondered what that might be. What had hurt him. If he'd hurt me. No. He wouldn't. He couldn't.

This was an exchange. Not an even one, either. I didn't get on my knees for anyone.

Why was I doing this? Why was I even considering Jed's bold offer? Because for the first time… ever, I wasn't controlled by my father. I didn't have to consider repercussions or how my actions could be used against me. How he could not only mess with me, but with Jed, too.

That was why I'd shut the casket, proving that he wasn't coming out of that thing and soon he'd be beneath six feet of dirt.

If I wanted to have Jed Barnett get me off, I could.

No strings. Sure, it was insane and perhaps stupid, but I was allowed to be both right about now.

He stepped close, so close I could feel his heat. His hand came up and he stroked my cheek again, his eyes following the move. I tried not to step back. Refused to do so. I wouldn't let him know he made me nervous, that long ago I'd thought about this, hoped for his touch.

"I'm not sleeping with you," I said. It was one thing to do this, another to go that far. I just... couldn't.

This close I could see the corner of his mouth turn up. I picked up his scent. Wintergreen and pine forests. "Who said anything about sleeping?" he murmured, his voice tipped low as if we were in a bubble where it was only the two of us.

"I'm not riding your dick," I clarified.

"You always make the rules?" His fingers slid through my hair, tucked the strands behind my ear. His touch was gentle. I expected him to turn us around, bend me over my father's desk and say *Who's your daddy now?*

"Always," I snapped, lifting my chin.

"We're not doing this here," he said, glancing around.

"Yes, we are."

"Your bedroom would be more private."

I wasn't having memories of Jed Barnett in my room. I'd have to relocate to one of the other nine bedrooms instead of spending the rest of my life remembering what I couldn't have.

"No one's going to bother us in here," I said, making it a fact. A given for how this was going to go. He stepped back, gave me room. I took a breath. I was rarely flustered, but I'd never been offered sex—no, orgasms—before. A guy had tried to pick me up in a bar a time or two, but that wasn't this. He'd caught me by surprise, and I didn't like surprises.

He nodded. "Your brothers going to be a problem?"

"You saw East. He's staying in the guest house with his sandwich. I haven't seen South and West, but they don't live here."

"Right, only you and your father in this big place." He stared up at the ceiling as if he could see through it like Superman.

"This is my house now. I do what I want."

His chin tipped down and he eyed me closely. "You fucking me in here to fuck your daddy over?"

I bristled. "One. We're not fucking. Two. *Macon,*" —I didn't call my father anything but his name and I made that clear now— "is dead. He's been involved in too much of my life." I left out the fact that he'd tried to sweeten a deal with my virginity and all the threats he'd made since. "If you can't keep my father out of what we're going to do, then it's not happening."

He studied me, either thinking I was completely insane or too rational, I wasn't sure. "Fair enough. Hand over the panties, princess."

He raised his hand between us, palm up.

I arched a brow, gave him a look that usually made men's balls shrivel. "I'm supposed to listen to you?"

He sighed. "We can do this with your panties on if you want."

"You didn't answer my question."

He moved his hand now in a circle between us. "You're under a strange notion that you're in charge."

"I said I made the rules."

He took his Stetson off, tossed it on the desk behind me. "You did. The rules are," —he raised a finger to start ticking them off— "we're doing this in here." He raised another finger. "We're not sleeping together." And another. "You're not riding my dick." And a fourth. "I'm not mentioning Macon Wainright again. Did I get them all?"

I narrowed my eyes, angry that he'd read me well. Too well, because he had more than a good memory. He was *listening*. I turned to storm off, but he caught me about the waist and pulled me back against him. I felt every hard inch of his body, including the thick prod of his dick against my ass. His forearm banded beneath my breasts and his mouth was brushing along the side of my neck. "I'll follow your rules," he murmured. "But I'm in charge. Yes?"

He was asking for my consent. To do whatever he said. He'd heard me, met my demands. Could I meet his?

I nodded, whispered, "Yes."

"Good girl. Now you can take off those panties yourself or I'll rip them off. Your choice. See how nice I am?"

I shivered as his breath fanned my skin. I hadn't been held like this in… ever. I wasn't a virgin, but I didn't do this. Have random, hot sex. Or hot not-sex. I had a local service on speed dial. Being a billionaire had its perks and I took advantage of a stable of hot men who met me at a hotel. On my schedule. With my rules. We fucked. I paid. They left. No strings.

Jed didn't seem to want strings either, but I wasn't paying him. He'd volunteered. When his hand cupped my breast, my mind went blank and I'd have to think all this through later.

Now, I melted at the feel of him. His hardness against my softness. He felt… untamed. As if he was only keeping himself in control because of my rules.

"Which is it, princess?" His hand slid down my body, his rough fingertips brushing my thigh at the hem of my dress.

"What if I don't want this?" I asked, suddenly wary. I might be able to jab my four-inch heel into the top of his foot, but he was bigger and stronger. No one would come running if they heard me screaming. Not in this house.

"You and your shotgun emptied the house, princess. Told me to stay. I don't force myself on a woman. If you don't want this after all, saying no works just fine. Any time along the way."

I didn't move. I couldn't. I could barely breathe. I felt small, feminine. Dominated, and he hadn't done anything yet.

He raised a dark brow, let his gaze drop down over my body. "Are you saying no?"

I shook my head.

With that consent, his hand moved up my thigh

taking the bottom of my dress with it. It was cut slim, but it moved easily until it was over my hips.

With him so close behind me, he couldn't see anything, only feel. A finger hooked into the thin band of lace at my hip and tugged. It gave way as if made of tissue. His other hand settled at my other hip, did the same to that side and I felt the g-string brush my inner thighs before he dangled it before us.

"You've been walking around with that tiny scrap over your pussy all this time?"

I felt the hard punch of his dick as he spoke. He was as affected as me. Seeing my panties was a thing for him. His hand moved away, then came back to reach around and cup me. I had no idea where my panties went, but I bucked at the feel of his calloused fingers over my most delicate flesh.

"Easy," he murmured, nipping my ear. "You're like a wild mare. You only need a little taming."

I bristled at that, tensing in his hold. "Fuck you, Jed."

"Ah, ah," he chided. "You said no dick riding."

I growled.

"Shh," he whispered as he began to stroke me. "All bare and dripping. You need this, princess."

I shook my head, disagreeing. I didn't like how he

was controlling me, how easily I responded, so I resisted. "I don't need this at all."

Except I did. I *really* did.

He took a step forward, moving me with him and pressed me into the edge of the desk. With one hand still between my legs, the other pressed into my back, bending me forward. I set my hands on the cool surface to brace myself.

Jed nudged my legs apart with a foot. "Your pussy says otherwise."

"My pussy's not in charge of me," I snapped.

When he pulled his hand away, I stifled a whimper by biting my lip. But his hand found me again, this time from behind. He wasn't petting any longer.

He penetrated me with a thick finger, the action eased by how wet I was. I went up on my toes, stuck my butt out and gasped.

"That's a shame. This perfect pussy should be calling the shots. It needs attention."

He leaned over me then. I felt his jeans pressing into my bare bottom, his chest against my back so he once again was speaking right into my ear.

Licking it. Nipping at the lobe.

He fucked me with the finger, then added another, finding my clit with his thumb and working me. It felt so good. God, I was hot and tingly, my pussy being played by a virtuoso. And that made me pissed. Made me get back in my head because how dare he bend me to his will so easily.

"Where'd you go, princess?"

Even though I was flushed and panting, I resisted. "You're using me."

His fingers stilled inside me, and I whimpered.

"How the fuck is me rubbing your g-spot until you drip all over my hand using you?" he questioned.

"Why are you doing this? What do you want from me?" My voice was a whine, my emotions raw and exposed, like a nerve on a bad tooth. I stared at his Stetson, knew he wasn't a paper pusher. A rich CEO playing at being from Montana. Jed Barnett was a born and bred cowboy. Rugged and abrasive to the core.

"I'm giving, not taking, North." His voice was calm. Even. He'd lost that bossy rasp.

I shook my head, looked over my shoulder at him. "Everyone wants something."

His eyes flared in surprise, then narrowed, as if resolved to something. He thrust into me again with those skilled fingers, curling them over, yup, my g-spot, which no other guy had ever found before.

"If we're having this conversation while I'm finger fucking you, I'm not doing it right. You're going to come, princess. Unless you say the word no, you don't have a choice."

"I don't like being out of control."

"I can tell, but you are in control. You say no, this stops. You're sopping wet from this, from giving over. Nothing wrong with someone else taking charge of you. Your secret's safe with me."

His thumb found my clit again and I slapped the desk with my sweaty palm as my mind lost the fight. He was too skilled. It felt too good.

I was close, right on the brink. I hovered there, whimpered. Moaned.

"Give it to me," he whispered.

I shook my head. "I can't."

"You will," he urged.

I turned my head, met his dark gaze. Saw the desire there, the need driving him to satisfy me.

He thought I was fighting him. I was, or I had been before it felt too good, until I went with him wherever he was taking me.

"I *can't*," I repeated and after a second, he caught on.

I couldn't come from a man. Not like this. I'd never been able to. I had orgasms, but I had to give them to myself. Even a guy as seemingly skilled as Jed, my body couldn't get there. Some guys didn't even notice.

Others got pissed off, thinking I had to control even that, but if I wanted an orgasm, I had to give it to myself. That was why I ditched men except for escorts. Men who did whatever I wanted and didn't get pissed when I got myself off while they were fucking me

Except Jed.

"Can you come on your own?"

I nodded.

Jed grabbed my right wrist and brought it down between me and the desk, set my hand over my pussy. "Get yourself there. I'll help." I felt his fingers inside me, parting me, then moved back so I was over my clit.

As he kept at my g-spot, rubbing and pressing in some magical way, I worked my clit with my fingers, circling it in just the right way that I knew worked.

"Fuck, that's so hot," he said, which broke away the shame and spurred me to come.

I tossed my head back, moaned low and deep as the orgasm hit me. The g-spot stimulation combined with my clit being worked was so intense. My palm slipped on the desk and Jed lifted me up, held me as I came and came.

Only when I sagged into his hold did he slip his fingers from me. My own were damp and sticky from touching myself, my brow sweaty.

He held me as I caught my breath.

"Again," he murmured. This time, when he spun me about and lifted me up so I sat on the desk, I didn't object. When he put a hand between my breasts and had me lay back on the hard surface, my dress up around my waist, I didn't say a word. When he lifted my heels up and over his shoulders and knelt on the floor, I only moaned. Then I grabbed his hair and held on for the ride as he took me with his mouth, totally okay with me helping with my fingers.

A few hours later, when my brothers and I buried my father in the family cemetery, the minister remarked on how relaxed I looked.

Maybe Jed was right. Orgasms sanctioned by God were the way to go.

3

JED

I PUSHED into Marshall's office and dropped into the chair across from him. Removed my hat. He was behind his desk and on the phone. I lifted my foot and crossed it over to my opposite knee, leaned back into a slouch and took on my usual air of indifference.

That wasn't faked.

I was thirty minutes late for our scheduled weekly meeting. Intentionally.

John Marshall was known in some circles as a hero. A saver of jobs. Revitalizing towns. In reality, he hired people to destroy the state. Logging, drilling, mining, fracking. If it hurt the planet, he was doing it.

Sure, it brought in jobs to remote towns, but while doing that work, men and women were polluting the water their kids drank. Depleting their natural resources, disturbing the ecosystem. The paycheck might put food in their kids' bellies, but when those kids grew up, there'd be nothing left to stay for.

He was killing Montana.

And he was getting away with it.

He didn't care about laws. All he got was a fine and then went back to work. It helped to have allies.

Allies like Macon Wainright who owned more land than anyone else in the state. That, and a shit ton of money, gave him power.

They'd gotten together and made deals. Pretty much Marshall did Wainright's dirty work.

I hadn't been back to Montana for more than a week at a time, other than for my parents' funeral, since I went to college. I'd lived in Virginia or DC and forgotten how special the Big Sky state really was.

The quiet. No rat race. Open land as far as the eye could see. Hell, even family.

Until this undercover op. I was "back" for good now, or that's what it seemed like to everyone. Maybe even me, too.

I was replacing rotting trim on the house. Fixing broken fences. Oiling squeaky doors. Everything that had been neglected because the house had been sitting empty. I *liked* it here. Now that I'd seen North, touched her, I was screwed.

Fuck. What a mess. I licked my lips remembering her taste and wondering if it was the last I was going to get.

The FBI had been interested in Wainright for everything from public corruption—bribing local and state officials, or even threatening them—to white collar crimes like money laundering and other fun stuff. If North knew about it all, then I was going to put her in handcuffs. If she was innocent, then I was going to be the shady asshole as soon as she did a little digging.

My cell vibrated in my pocket and since Marshall was occupied, I pulled it out. My boss.

Need an update on the delivery of the fence posts.

To any Montanan who read the text, it seemed like I was tackling a summer project. To me, it meant Director Amy Sprouse wanted me to check in about what I'd learned from making contact with North. I met Marshall's eyes even as he spoke on the phone. That was why I was here in his office.

An update. It seemed my boss would have to wait in line.

Finally, Marshall slammed the phone back in its

cradle, then set his forearms on his desk and eyed me. He was sixty, overweight, balding. He looked like Wimpy from *Popeye.* All that was missing was the little brown hat. Sweat dotted his forehead, even in the air-conditioned building.

"Well?" he asked, his bushy eyebrows going up.

"You want a play by play?" I asked.

I saw the disgusting interest in his eyes.

"I'm surprised she spread her legs for a guy like you."

Since everyone in the area knew I'd been recruited out of college by the FBI—small town life had its drawbacks—that couldn't be hidden as part of an undercover persona. I had a past they couldn't alter. So the feds created a new version of my present. The story went that I'd planned to take payouts from the bad guys I'd been trying to catch. While those bad guys had been caught and convicted because of it and other shady shit, I'd been fired in disgrace. Because I had close to twenty years of service and I actually hadn't done anything illegal... yet, I hadn't been convicted along with them. Returning to Montana with my tail between my legs, I now managed my parents' ranch.

Some carefully placed clues about my return and

Marshall had hired me on. Corrupt hired corrupt. I'd been undercover ever since.

That made me tied to Marshall and North's father. In bad ways. I did Marshall's dirty work; handling deals with guys like Wainright that destroyed the state. Killed wildlife, cut down forests.

It was obvious North hadn't caught on to that part yet. If she had she'd have blown a hole in me with that shotgun instead of letting me go down on her.

It was one thing for me to think about her bent over her father's desk, another for Marshall to disrespect her by that shit talk. North wasn't a cheap hooker he fucked in a shady motel. I hadn't figured her out yet, but she didn't deserve those words.

I hadn't stopped thinking about her in the two days since her daddy's wake and funeral. Two days since I had my fingers inside her, my mouth on her pussy.

I still felt her walls ripple around me. Saw the panic in her eyes when I'd gotten her close to coming, then the frustration when she couldn't make it happen.

I was man enough to have her work her clit until she came. Oh, I'd make her come without any help. Soon. But then? In that moment? The goal wasn't to break her, it was to take the edge off, because it didn't seem like she had any opportunity to do so.

Did she ever have fun? Did she ever let down that guard of hers?

She was so in her head. That was why, when she did come, it was so fucking incredible. The way she let go, gave herself over to me even for a few seconds.

I'd get that again. I'd get everything from her because now that I knew what she looked like when she let go completely. When she gave herself to me.

Because she was going to be mine.

He sat back, laughed. "It's like that, is it?"

I gritted my back teeth. Realized my goal of having North Wainright was going to be a complicated one. I couldn't let on that I was truly interested in her.

"I'm not a kid. What I do with my dick is my business," I snapped, trying to redirect him.

"As long as you *do* North Wainright."

"You want her to talk. You want me to get her to do that. How I accomplish it is not up for question."

How was I going to get him the info he wanted while I got the woman?

He held up his hands as if to ward me off. "I have millions sunk into this deal which means I want updates. You can leave your dick out of the report."

That was all the flex he was going to give.

"I was at her father's wake," I reminded. "It's not like she was in the mood to talk business."

"That woman is *all* business."

I thought that too. The dress, the heels. The cold attitude. If I hadn't gotten under her skirt, I'd have wondered if she had a set of balls.

I'd been in Marshall's "employment" for three months. In that time, I'd gotten in front of Macon Wainright but hadn't been able to collect proof of his dirty deeds. The guy had been an asshole and trusted no one. Not even his daughter. That was why the feds put me undercover with Marshall instead. To get to Wainright that way. It had worked, but then he'd died. It had been un-fucking-believable hearing about it. Fifty-five and a massive coronary.

I'd thought the case over, but no. My boss had only moved me toward a new source.

North.

"I need to see this deal done. I was supposed to be in and out. Wainright being dead is fucking everything up. I bought that land for him, and he has to pay me for it." He stuck out his finger and pointed it at me like Uncle Sam. "North does."

He'd bought up a huge parcel at the Canadian border that Wainright wanted. The deal was that

Wainright was going to buy it off him—at a higher value which was Marshall's payment for his involvement—for a nature preserve. A huge tax write off for Wainright Holdings. But from what Marshall had told me, a logging company was waiting in the wings to lease the land and raze the pristine forest that sat upon it. Strip mining and other shit once the trees were out of the way. The profit for Wainright was to be huge.

"So much for a nature preserve," I muttered.

Marshall sputtered. "Nature preserve? Who gives a fuck about nature. I want that land sold. I want my money!" He slapped his hand on the desk.

"Why do you have such a hard on about this deal with Wainright? Your check will be cut from the Wainright Holdings' philanthropic arm."

He snorted, which was not a pretty sound. "Which is run by North. She learns the truth about her daddy's plans, and she'll shut it all down. That girl's got her momma's green agenda even though that woman's been dead for over twenty years, which is a big fucking problem. Who cares about the spotted owl or the wolf?"

He was a fucking dick. "You don't know if she's going to bail on the sale or not," I said, confirming.

"It's your job to ensure that woman signs on the line."

He looked at me with narrowed eyes. I assumed he was trying to look threatening, but it wasn't working.

"It's her business silo. The company's "giving back" was started by her. They're known for their philanthropy. She's got to know about this."

Based on what I'd figured out about her, she knew everything that was going on at work. Not only for Marshall, but for the FBI, I had to find out how much the new CEO was involved in Marshall's deal. Because she might be in just as deep as her dead daddy.

That meant she'd be doing serious jail time and I'd be the one putting on the handcuffs. I didn't understand myself, why I still wanted her if she was possibly guilty. Ever since I saw her at the wake, my dick had been in charge, which meant I might be in big trouble. I couldn't resist her.

I stood. There was no reason to linger. I'd given him my update, which was nothing. He'd blustered and tried to scare me into doing a better job. All it told me was Marshall was guilty as hell and we had his land deal to prove it. He'd go down, but not until we had Macon Wainright posthumously pinned for his crimes. I just wasn't sure if his daughter would be joining them.

"I'm on it."

That's all I said as I put my hat back on and left his office.

4

NORTH

"YOU HAVE a call with Mark Andres at eleven, lunch at the rotary at twelve, a meeting with the board at two. Accounting wants to be squeezed in sometime so they have a five minute spot before your three o'clock call with the cattlemen's association."

My assistant, Julian, recounted my day as he stared at his tablet. It was my second day back at the office since the funeral and I was as booked as ever.

I was at my desk. It wasn't the corner office, but the space was big. I swiveled my chair around to look out the windows. The view was north, the buildings of Billings and then the brown buttes and crags in the distance. I was on the fourth floor, and I could see for miles. I could take over the huge corner office that had been my father's, but I had no interest. That space was tainted, just like everything else he touched.

"You have the board's agenda?"

"In your inbox," he replied.

I had to reassure the group that while things were going to change at Wainright Holdings, it was all going to be for the better. The company had been under my father's ruthless thumb for too long. It was finally time to steer it the way I wanted. There were going to be some holdouts, those who were still loyal to my father even though it was unwarranted. They were no longer going to get favors or perks or bonuses. They could vote me out as CEO even though I was the primary stakeholder, but my brothers and I combined held more than fifty percent. I wasn't being replaced because South, East, and West wanted nothing to do with the place.

"I need you to start to merge my father's meetings in with my own. Connect with Janice," —his assistant who was ridiculously loyal, meaning he'd either been fucking her or well-compensating her, or both— "to make it happen."

"I have. The first one should be here any minute." He didn't tell me there weren't enough hours in the day for two schedules worth of meetings, but it had to be done. I had to tackle Macon's business and make it my own and I studied my calendar on my tablet trying to figure out how to make it all fit.

"Call Mrs. Sanchez and coordinate a moving company to empty my father's bedroom completely. All the furniture, clothes. Donate it to a charity."

The woman had been the ranch's housekeeper for over a decade. She handled the cleaning staff, the cook, food. Anything that happened inside the main house, she dealt with so I didn't have to.

I'd work through the rest of the house later, like figuring out how to get rid of all those animal head trophies while honoring the animals' lives needlessly taken solely for my father's amusement. It wasn't as if he'd eaten the meat from any of those kills. At least someone in need would be wearing his clothes and shoes. My father would be rolling over in his grave. He'd probably rather burn the expensive things instead of seeing someone else use them. Perhaps it was payback what I was doing, but it felt hollow. Like I was never going to win.

"On it," Julian said, not even blinking at the request. "Dinner with your brothers at the ranch means I've scheduled your ride for five-fifteen."

"Right." East hadn't returned to Bozeman but had

been scarce. All three of them had, which wasn't a surprise. We'd all decided to hang tonight before he left.

"Can I help you?"

I spun my chair around at Julian's question. There in the open doorway was Jed Barnett. My pussy clenched at the sight of him. God, he was handsome. Now that I knew what he was like—intense, demanding, surprisingly gentle—I was excited to see him.

Not that I'd let him pick up on that.

The last thing I needed was a man who thought they could walk all over me. Even one who gave me incredible orgasms.

I stood. "What are you doing here?"

The corner of his mouth tipped up as his gaze raked over me. I wore a dress, as usual, this time in a forest green. He couldn't see the matching heels behind the desk.

"I'm your nine o'clock," Jed said. That deep rasp made my nipples harden.

Come. I remembered how that one word he'd murmured in my ear sounded. I didn't like to be bossed around but found it hot when he did it.

I looked to my assistant who looked a little surprised Jed had snuck up on him. No one got past his desk... usually. I was coming to understand that Jed Barnett was different.

He looked relaxed in that casual way that screamed he had no fucks to give. That it didn't matter that Julian was my gatekeeper. He was coming in anyway.

Jed's boots were polished, but his jeans were worn, which only meant they molded to his thick thighs and butt... and package that much better. His shirt today was red plaid with the sleeves rolled up.

After I took a blatant few seconds just to ogle him, I realized he was the first appointment Julian had mentioned.

"You had a meeting with my father," I said, tipping my chin up.

"I did."

Two words that changed everything. No one had a meeting with Macon Wainright for fun. It had been all business, all the time.

Which meant his laser focus at the wake had been intentional. A plan of his that had me bent over my father's desk.

The plan had worked, too.

"Thanks, Julian," I said, dismissing him but not looking away from Jed.

Julian gave Jed a bland look before shutting the door behind him.

I stood, refusing to look anything but powerful. I'd learned one didn't sit when others were standing. "You're an asshole."

All he did was quirk a brow as I came around the desk.

"What was my dad's plan?" I asked.

"To die so I'd come onto you at his wake?" he asked, making me sound ridiculous.

I shook my head. "You had opportunity, so you took it."

It was subtle, but I noticed the way his jaw clenched. Just for a second. Fuck.

"Let me guess. The plan was to fuck me so I'd be distracted and miss some deal for a crony? Get me to fall in love with you, and then what? That's a little extreme, but I've seen my father in action."

He frowned but stayed quiet.

I paced back and forth and considered all the options. It gave me a minute to pull myself together, to try not to let him see how much of a fool I felt. I'd thought of him for two days. How he'd touched me. How he hadn't gotten his male pride dented because I couldn't come without doing it myself. For a short time there, I'd thought he was different.

"Or is it because the deal with your dad fell through when I was seventeen and Macon's been trying again?"

"What the fuck are you talking about?" he asked.

I ignored him. All these ideas had me on a path to the truth. I stilled, realizing what it was. "It wasn't him. It was you. You came to the wake because you want payback for what I did to your brother."

"You done?" He took off his hat, tossed it onto a chair, but didn't look away from me. "There's a lot to unpack here. You think your daddy sent me to fuck you?"

I crossed my arms, leaned against my desk.

He studied me, narrowed his eyes, seemingly figuring out what he wanted from my lack of response. Moving close, he crowded me, setting his hands on the wooden surface on either side of my hips. It brought his face right in front of mine. I could see the red in his beard, the depth of his gaze.

I swallowed. Refused to look away. I would not show weakness.

I didn't see anger there precisely. It was something, but it didn't seem directed at me.

"I'll take your silence as a yes. The fact that you even suggested it means he's done it before. I remember my parents had a deal for their land that fell through, but I was in DC at the time. I never heard more about it before they died. There is no deal now with your father, princess. The land's mine. I'd know."

"Then why are you here?" I asked.

He didn't step back, didn't give me room. I wasn't afraid of him, but he made me uneasy. Uncomfortable, because he was actually looking at me. Seeing me. Hell, *hearing* my words.

"I work for Marshall Industries. Your daddy did have a deal going. With them. I'm here to see it done."

I blinked, surprised. I knew John Marshall. Total sleaze. I hadn't expected Jed to work for him, but I hadn't thought much about him besides how talented he was with his hands. How he smelled. How incredible he could kiss.

I should've looked into Jed, but I hadn't. A stupid mistake on my part.

"And you thought you'd do that at the wake while I was bent over a desk?"

"Jesus, you've got issues. I went to the wake to pay my respects to the family. *Maybe* talk about the deal. But one look at you and that all changed. I might've kept my distance when you were a kid, but not any longer."

My mouth fell open. He'd wanted me all those years ago.

"What?" I whispered.

"You heard me. I want you and I take what I want."

I wasn't sure if I should be insulted at the way he was talking about me or turned on. The way my panties were getting wet, it was definitely the latter.

"I... I can't go over the Marshall deal with you. I don't know the details since I haven't caught up on my father's work," I admitted, as if that explained why my thoughts had gone the directions they had. Although I'd given away more than I wanted.

He pushed off the desk, stepped back. "That's fine. We can meet another time to go over it, answer any questions you have about the contract. In the meantime, I have a deal of my own." He picked up his hat, dropped into the chair. "Between you and me."

His long legs crowded me so I went around my desk, sat across from him. Had this been his plan? "Land? Cattle? A loan?"

His gaze narrowed. "Holy fuck, princess. Everyone's after you for something, aren't they?"

"Aren't you?" I countered, leaning back in my chair, wary and suddenly feeling fragile. I'd let him in the other day and I hadn't thought through the *why* of it. Not then and not the time since. An error on my part.

He shifted forward, rested his forearms on his thighs, as if following me, not wanting to lose any space between us. "You forget who got off the other day? It sure as shit wasn't me."

I frowned. His dick hadn't come out of his pants. He hadn't asked for a handy or a BJ. Nothing.

I blinked. Lost. "I... I don't understand."

"Yeah, I can see that. Okay, here's what we're going to do. I'm going to teach you to trust someone. To let those huge fucking walls down because that version of you I saw the other day, no thought in her head, no worries, only pleasure, was the prettiest fucking thing I've ever seen."

I blushed. I couldn't help it. My cheeks heated and it spread down my torso. All of me warmed by his words. His intense stare.

Was he actually telling the truth?

"Why?" I asked. "Why are you doing this? You have to have a reason."

"You mean an ulterior motive."

I raised my hands, frustrated. "Everyone does."

"Not everyone."

We stared at each other. I was... caught. He made no sense. He wasn't like other men. I had no idea what to expect from him, especially when he said he had no ulterior motive for wanting me.

"The deal is what? To be my fuck buddy? No thanks, I already have one."

His eyes narrowed. His jaw clenched.

"You have a boyfriend?" The words were laced with ice, as if angry he'd put his hands on a woman who was claimed.

I laughed, not because it seemed he had honor, but because the idea of me having a boyfriend was hilarious. The last one I had was his brother. Thirteen years ago.

"No. A no strings scheduled appointment for sex."

His eyes widened and he looked at me as if I'd sprouted devil horns.

"That's pretty fucking sad."

I bristled. If he intended to hurt me with that, he had. "Why is it that a woman can't get what she wants without attachment?" I practically snapped.

"There's nothing wrong with that, but that's not you."

I laughed at the idea he knew more about me than I did. "Oh yes, it is."

He stood, loomed over me. "No, it's not. You want sex, you get it from someone who thinks of you as more than a transaction. And not any of those vibrators you mentioned either."

I tipped my head to the side. "And that's you?"

"I see you, princess."

I froze. My breath caught. I didn't even blink. *He*

sees me. I wasn't sure if that was good or the scariest thing ever, because no one saw me.

Ever.

I licked my lips and his dark gaze dropped to watch the motion. "What... what are you proposing?"

Fuck, I hated there was a catch in my voice.

"That pussy's mine." He looked down as if he could see it through my desk. "Hell, I don't even know why we're having this conversation. You gave it to me the other day. I don't share. No fucking way can you go off and see some... escort now."

He was right. I craved him and I hadn't done that... ever. Had I been longing for him all this time? Had I always wanted Jed Barnett since the first time I saw him?

Maybe I gave away some emotion or he was somehow a pussy whisperer because the corner of his mouth tipped up.

"We'll fuck until you get tired of me. Your rules, princess."

My eyes widened. "My rules?"

He outright grinned now. His straight white teeth stood out against his dark beard. "Your rules, but I'm in charge, remember? I'm going to break down every one of those walls you've built up. Now give me those panties."

I looked around, as if the people working for me could see through the closed door. "What?"

He came around the desk, tugged so I stood directly before him, then turned so I was caught between him and my desk.

"You don't trust. I can see that."

"I—" He put a finger over my lips.

"You need to trust me on one thing. That I won't hurt you."

That was a big one. He wouldn't hurt me? Who hadn't? Even my brothers, unknowingly.

"Not in this. You trust me with your body, with your pleasure. I'll keep you safe. No one will harm you when you're with me. No one will see you. See the person you're trying so fucking hard to protect."

He pulled his finger away, but I couldn't tell him to fuck off. I couldn't do anything but say his name.

His eyes flared because he heard the weakness in my voice. The… hope that he wasn't lying.

"I don't know what this is between us," he added. "No fucking clue, but I'm not afraid to find out. Give over, because I have. Give over, North, because you like it."

He said my name instead of princess.

Again, he somehow *saw* me when he looked at me. As if I was more than just a Wainright. More than just my bank account. My land. My inherited power.

I had no idea what this was between us either. I felt it. Electricity. Chemistry. Something unexplainable and intangible. I couldn't grab the feeling, but I could reach for him. Hope he'd catch me because I felt like I was falling.

I was the new North Wainright. I was no longer under my father's thumb. Word wouldn't get back to him that Jed had been in my office for the past ten minutes. That we were going to start something, something that didn't have an agenda. Because it didn't even make sense.

My father wasn't going to hold it against me, blackmail me with it.

"Okay."

He'd been patiently waiting. When his eyes flared with surprise, it seemed he was expecting me to say no. To knee him in the balls or smash the top of his foot with my stiletto. Anything but submit.

Leaning in, he kissed me. It was the lightest brush of his lips against mine, then he pulled back. "Now give me those panties."

"I'm not having sex with you in my office," I said.

"If that's a rule, fine. But if you're saying no because you think you're in charge, then I'm shutting that shit down now. If I want you on your knees sucking me off right here, you will. If I want to bend you over your desk, I will."

"You're an asshole," I muttered, but didn't argue.

He caught on to that because he said, "Maybe, but I make you wet. Wanna know why?"

I only arched a brow. Boy, did I want to hear this. "Because you like it when I tell you what to do. But I'd never do anything to hurt or humiliate you, including letting anyone in your office see you in a way you consider weak. Remember, while you might get on your knees for me, princess, you hold all the power."

I stared at him. He was right. I could kick him out. Tell him no. Hell, have him arrested for some stupid charge because my last name held a lot of power. Whatever we did was on me.

"Yeah, you're smart," he continued. "You know exactly what I mean. Now give me those panties."

He stepped back and I lost his heat.

Inwardly, I grumbled. Planned his demise. Hated his guts. All the while I reached beneath my dress and tugged my panties down and off, then handed them over.

He stared at the lavender lace, so feminine in his long, work-worn fingers, then tucked it into his shirt pocket.

"I'll see you later, princess."

I watched as he cut across the room.

"Wait! That's it?" I bit my lip, realizing I sounded desperate. I didn't *do* desperate because it made me appear weak. And the weak were preyed upon. Still, I had to know. "You expect me to... to just go without panties at work?"

He winked. "You won't be able to think about anything else. See you around."

With that, he turned and left. I stared at the open doorway, a little confused about what just happened as I felt cool air on my pussy. His pussy, the one that was very, very wet.

I went to the door, spoke to Julian. "Get me everything there is on Jed Barnett. And find out what deal my father had with John Marshall."

5

JED

"WHAT HAPPENED between you and North Wainright?" I asked, adjusting my grip on my steering wheel. I had my cell in a stand on my dash, set to speaker as I drove out of town.

"North?" my brother asked. "God, that was a long time ago."

I might have her panties tucked into my pocket, but I didn't know much about the woman. And I'd looked. Online searches through the various FBI databases didn't give me much. She had a driver's license and had several cars registered to her name, but to get from the ranch to the main office in Billings in a reasonable time, she took a helicopter.

A fucking helicopter. Meaning no speeding or parking tickets.

We couldn't access the corporate emails or files without a warrant, and I couldn't serve her one without blowing my cover. She didn't have any accounts on social media and her personal emails were limited to connecting with those who worked for the family. The Wainrights had a ranch manager who handled the land and the outbuildings. That was a huge job and had seven full-time on staff. Cutting grass in the summer, plowing snow the rest of the year, mending fences, running the stables. There was also a house manager, a woman who took care of everything inside the Wainright home. And guest house. That included cleaners, a cook, hiring caterers for a wake, tackling maintenance issues. Probably even putting up holiday lights.

North didn't have the time to go to the store and pick up pretzels or toilet bowl cleaner. Someone fed her, made her bed, washed her clothes, serviced her car... hell, serviced her helicopter. From what she'd said, even serviced *her.*

It wasn't because she was an entitled bitch, but because she worked. All the fucking time.

The only thing I discovered was that she had a shoe buying problem. And since every pair I'd seen on her had four-inch heels, it was all done online. Those shoes weren't sold in Montana. I liked those heels. I liked her in them. I liked having them over my shoulders the other day.

I shifted in my seat.

"She broke up with you?" I asked Jock.

I could hear chattering in the background. It was either Tyler or Jamie, my nephews, and from the sound of water splashing, they were in the tub. For a family with small kids, it was bath time.

"She did," he said.

"I thought you two had been hot and heavy." The thought of her with Jock made me see red, even though it had been over a decade ago. At the wake, she'd said she'd been surprised I wanted my younger brother's sloppy seconds. That meant they'd fucked.

I'd spent the day tracking down the escort service she used for her *no strings scheduled appointment for sex.* I didn't think she'd lied when telling me that. What woman would share that and it be a lie?

I'd called the service, saying I was her assistant, Julian, and cancelled all her standing appointments. She wasn't seeing *Brad* ever again, not with me around to give her whatever she needed.

When I'd told the woman Miss Wainright was now in a relationship, she'd been pleased for her. Unlike North, who when she found out what I'd done, would want to cut out my spleen with a butter knife.

"Hot and heavy for seventeen," he replied. "I guess. We went on dates. The lake. Ice cream at Dot's. Hell, even bowling. I wasn't a high school Casanova. What is it you're wanting to know?"

"She said her father had a deal going with Mom and Dad."

"You saw her?"

"I went to the wake." I wasn't going to offer more than that. Unfortunately, to make my cover as legit as possible, Jock thought I'd been kicked out of the FBI and that I was working for John Marshall. He wasn't thrilled about it. No one around here liked Marshall. But I was forty and he didn't have much say in what I did.

We were pretty close, especially since our parents had been killed in a car accident and we were the only family we had, but I was ten years older. I'd left for college when he was still in elementary school so there was a lot we didn't know about each other.

"I heard Macon Wainright died," he said. "Man, he was an ass—special kind of guy." One of the kids laughed followed by a huge splash.

"Ass! Ass!"

Jock groaned. "Tyler, don't let your mother hear you say that. And leave the water in the tub."

I turned off the main road and headed east.

"I went once, to Billionaire Ranch, to pick her up," Jock continued. "Macon opened the door, offered me a beer."

He offered a seventeen-year-old kid who was going to be driving his daughter a *beer?*

"I first thought it was a test and told him no. But he'd been serious. You'd think he wanted to know what time I'd be bringing his daughter home, not getting me drunk."

"Yeah." I had no idea what else to say.

"First, he told me how he was real friendly with Mom and Dad. Then... get this." I could hear him laugh through the phone. "He gave me a strip of condoms. Told me that while fucking North was fine and all but making him a granddaddy wasn't."

"Daddy said a bad word! Ass! Fuck!"

"Holy shit," I mumbled, and not about my nephew's growing vocabulary.

"No kidding. I had no choice but to take the things, tuck them in my pocket. After that I'd been too scared to do more than kiss North."

"You never slept with her?" I was surprised and I was sure it sounded in my voice.

"Laugh at me and I'll kill you, but I couldn't get it up. I mean, all I could think about was her dad practically giving me his blessing to fuck her."

I could imagine. A teenager's dick got hard all the time, and around a pretty, young North, it would be impossible to keep it down. Except for what Macon had done.

So North's words at the wake had been tossed out in anger. In self-defense?

"Now that I'm older, I have to wonder if he was using reverse psychology or some shit like that."

No. I doubted that. Macon had wanted Jock to have sex with North.

If he wasn't dead, I'd want to beat the shit out of him, because I had a feeling the reason why was going to piss me off. The only one alive to know the answer was North.

"She break up with you because you couldn't perform?" What little I knew of her, I doubted that was the case.

"I never took it that far. Like I said, all I could see was her dad. She was sweet. Her laugh was... infectious. Besides her being gorgeous, I just liked her. Then one day, she came over and broke up with me. This was after the condom thing, not that she knew about it. She was upset but wouldn't tell me why. Said we were going away to college and that it wasn't going to work out."

"That's it? She gave you the 'It's not you, it's me?'" I stared blankly at the road out the window.

"I guess, but I remember clearly the next day the deal for the ranch fell through."

I slowed for the metal cattle guard that went across the dirt road. "You remember that?"

"Oh yeah. We were headed to San Diego to celebrate, using some of the money. Mom canceled the trip."

I remembered that. The phone call with my dad telling me they'd decided not to sell the ranch after all. I'd been busy with work, putting in tons of hours out of Quantico, and hadn't asked too many questions. They hadn't tried to sell it to anyone else after that. Then they'd died, leaving the property to me and Jock. He'd gotten married the next year I'd bought him out of his half. He'd gone and bought a place in Bozeman near his wife's family.

I'd come home for vacations, only returning permanently as part of my cover. In my down time, I was fixing the place up.

I slowed when I came upon the huge wooden arch

with Wainright Ranch carved into it. The place had been nicknamed Billionaire Ranch for as long as I could remember. No one called it by anything else.

The drive was paved and meandered across the rolling landscape. The house sat back almost a mile from the road.

"Thanks, Jock. Tell Ellen hi for me and kiss the kids."

"Come down soon and do it yourself," he countered.

"Will do."

I ended the call and turned down the drive and stewed over what Jock had shared. He never slept with North. What had she said in her office earlier? That maybe I'd gotten together with her father as payback for what she did to Jock. That made no sense. Based on what my brother had just told me, she hadn't done anything to him. She assumed I'd connected with her father before he died and had… offered her up as part of a deal? That I was at his wake to collect?

Did that mean he'd offered her up to Jock when they were kids to sweeten the deal with his parents?

I pulled into the circular drive, parked, ran a hand over my face.

What the fuck was wrong with me? Getting with North Wainright wasn't a simple thing. Hell, she had to be the most complex woman I'd ever met. She had issues. A fuck ton of them, even though she had enough money to solve every single one of them. I looked up at the huge house that proved that.

I was a glutton for punishment because my dick wanted her. My head wanted her too. There was something about her. Something... complex and intriguing.

I was surprised, at my age, that I could spend all my time thinking about a woman, but I did. How she was the last fucking woman on the planet who I should get a hard on for.

She might be seriously guilty of federal crimes.

She was now the number one focus of my case.

And I wanted her to be... what? Mine?

I sighed, grabbed my hat off the seat. Yeah, I did.

Except when she found out I was undercover, it wasn't going to end well. I even knew how well she could shoot, and I still wanted her.

It still didn't matter. It was rare to find a woman that made life interesting. She was also damaged and from what I could tell, had no one on her side. Oh, she had a shit ton of people working for her, to do whatever she wanted. Even *Brad.*

But they weren't watching out for her. They helped because she was paying them.

I walked up the broad stone steps to the front door. Rang the bell as I took in the grand entry.

She was a princess alone in her big fucking castle. Was I her prince? Far from it, but I was going to be there for her. To figure out what made her tick. What made her smile. And give that to her for the rest of her life. As I thought that, I should have panicked. Hopped back in my truck and drove off, dirt flying. But no, it sounded about perfect.

When I heard the gunshot, I wondered if I might be too late.

6

NORTH

BESIDES THE FUNERAL, where we all confirmed our father had definitely been put in the ground, my brothers and I hadn't been together for dinner since Christmas. That was because Macon had been in Cabo with his mistress and the only time the guys came to the house was when he was gone.

The last time they had slept beneath the roof was the night before each of them went to college. They'd gone off and never come back.

Yeah, it had been that much of a shit show.

We talked on the phone, at least once a week, and I saw West and South about once a month, either at one of their places or in town. Never at the house.

"Who wants another?" East called out, holding up the whiskey bottle in one hand and had a shotgun hinged open and tucked under his other arm.

"Me," South and West said at the same time.

West pulled the string on the trap and a glass ashtray went flying. South aimed and fired his own weapon and blew the ashtray to pieces over the field.

We were wearing hearing protection, so they shouted.

I'd been out here shooting the longest, somehow returning from the office before any of them arrived. The helicopter was sitting in its usual spot on the west lawn.

I'd gone inside to change my clothes as usual, passed a wall of all of Macon's trophies and other memorabilia. I'd stopped, realized I hated every piece of it. The gloating, the self-adoration. I'd grabbed as much as I could carry off the wall and took it out back, only returning for the shotgun, some shells from his office and trading my heels for a pair of rain boots in the mud room.

I'd set the items on the top of the split rail fence at the back edge of the garden and took aim. That was where my brothers found me. They'd collected more of his things and an extra shotgun and decided to make it more fun by using the skeet trap, so we'd moved to the field. East had also grabbed a bottle of whiskey.

He passed the liquor and grabbed a silver plate, read the inscription. "Man Of The Year 2011. More like Asshole of the Year," he added.

He glared as if it held all the shitty memories of that time, then walked over to the trap, set it in place, then loaded shells into the gun.

I moved to take his spot, waited for him to get in position and give me the nod. I pulled the rope and a split second later, he fired. The plate pinged in the air, then went flying like an out of control UFO in the direction of the stables.

"Fuck you, Macon!" he shouted.

Yeah, fuck you.

South grabbed another silver plate and flung it like a frisbee. It got good air and landed just shy of the pond.

When someone came running around the side of the house, his footsteps on the flagstone walk loud even through the hearing protection, we all spun around.

Jed.

When he saw what we were up to, he came to a

skidding halt, then set his hands on his hips, gun in his right hand, taking a second to breathe.

"Jesus." I could barely hear him but read his lips.

I tugged out the hearing protection, let it dangle around my neck like an open necklace.

He tucked the gun into the back of his pants and stalked over in the same clothes as this morning. I watched his long-legged gait, the shift of his narrow hips, the way his muscles flexed beneath his jeans. If there was a picture of a cowboy in the dictionary, he'd be it.

Eddie got up from the spot where he'd been sleeping in the sunshine and approached. The dog hadn't even stirred from the shotgun blasts but wanted to greet Jed.

"Does everything you do involve shooting?" he asked, stepping close and stroking my hair back.

Lately. "I decided to get rid of some things," I answered. Macon's bedroom had been emptied as I'd asked.

He looked to the pile in the grass, then back at me. "I see that."

"I did some data mining on you. I'd say your time in the FBI probably made you a good shot," I said. He'd worked for them that summer I saw him at his parents' barbecue. Yet he'd been recently fired, although I hadn't gotten the details on that. He'd left the east coast behind and returned to the family ranch. And a job with John Marshall.

"I can hold my own," he replied.

"You always walk around with a gun?" I said, glancing at the holstered weapon on his hip.

He gave me a questioning look. "Says the woman who shoots up a wake. This is Montana, everyone has a gun."

Eddie nudged his thigh and Jed looked down, gave him a scratch behind his ear. The dog leaned into Jed's leg, closing his eyes. Yeah, I knew the feeling. Those fingers were magic.

"We were just reminiscing," East said as he came over, pointing to where he just shot the commemorative plate. "You knew Macon?"

Jed nodded.

"That asshole..." East cleared his throat and held up the plate so Jed could read the inscription. "Excuse me, *man of the year,* had me kicked off the varsity football team. That threatened my scholarship to State." He shook his head. "Fuck, I thought I was going to be stuck here baling hay the rest of my life."

Jed glanced around, taking in the house, the stables in the distance, probably trying to figure out why that would be such a hardship.

"I have no idea what made him change his mind," East continued.

South and West grumbled, went over and slapped East on the back. They did so as he took a swig of whiskey, which had him spilling some on his university t-shirt.

Macon's mind change? That had been me. I'd been a sophomore at Harvard. Macon had learned from when South had gone to college the year before that I'd do anything to set them free. I'd made a deal with the devil for South. Then he'd threatened both East and West the following year—without their knowledge, although to them it was only dick moves on his part to fuck with them. Like getting East kicked off the football team.

Their freedom had been at stake and since I'd already bargained my life away, I did whatever it took.

Almost.

When I realized Jed was watching me, I looked away. Afraid he could read my mind.

"You're the guy from the wake," East said.

Jed turned to him, introduced himself. They shook hands and East glanced between Jed and me, his face filled with curiosity.

"My other brothers West and South," I added.

"Don't ask us to line up in order," South said,

taking a pull of whiskey. He was the shortest of the three, at six feet.

"I'm sure you get that all the time," Jed commented.

"South's got our mother's maiden name," I explained. "Southforth. East and West are short for Easton and Weston."

They were twins, but fraternal. They didn't look or act anything alike. One was a rancher, the other a university professor. Although they were two years younger, they were six inches taller.

"And North?" he asked.

I shrugged. "Just North."

"Your father's sense of humor gave you those names?"

South shook his head. "Macon? He didn't have one. Our mother named us."

"What are you doing here?" I asked. We might be shooting up Macon's things, but I didn't want to talk about him.

The sun was moving lower in the sky, creating a soft haze over the prairie. There was barely any breeze.

My brothers turned back to the pile of Macon's things. West grabbed some kind of golf trophy, went over to the trap. East stood beside South, clearly they were content drinking and shooting at things for the next while.

"I told you I'd see you later," Jed said, turning my attention back to him. "Overheard you were having dinner with your brothers."

Ah, when he showed up at my office this morning.

"Why?" I started walking toward the house, leaving the guys to their fun. I'd lost interest.

"Wanted to meet them."

"Again, why?"

"Because they're the people you care about."

I pushed through the mudroom door, bent down to work off my rain boots.

"What did you do to get Macon to change his mind about East's school?" he wondered, and I caught him eyeing my ass.

I popped upright at his surprise question, the room spun. Jed took my arm. I was barefoot now, and our height difference was much more noticeable. I only came up to his shoulder.

There was no way I was going to tell him about the Texas oilman.

"I don't know what you're talking about."

Eddie pushed through the dog door, went to his beloved bed in the corner, circled three times, then flopped down.

"Yeah, you do. In your office earlier, you thought I'd made a deal with your daddy, your pussy sweetening the deal. No one makes up shit like that." He hadn't let go of his hold, his thumb stroking over my bare skin. "Your brothers got out of here. You didn't. Why's that?"

"Someone had to take over the business," I snapped. He was pissing me off. Getting too close to the truth.

He slowly shook his head.

"Try again."

Not happening. Instead, I said, "Look, this isn't going to work."

"What isn't?" he asked.

I heard the boom of the shotgun, meaning my brothers were far away and occupied. Still, I didn't want any of them to be a part of this.

I stormed out of the room, cut into the salon where the bar cart was beside the grand piano my grandfather had bought my grandmother and grabbed a bottle of whiskey. The household staff not only kept the house immaculate, but fully stocked of anything Macon or I could ever want.

Right now, I wanted to get completely drunk. Forget my brothers were here. While I loved them dearly, seeing them reminded me that they would leave after dinner and go back to their lives. Real lives. Happy ones, full of dreams fulfilled. Rainbows and unicorns and all that. Forget that Jed had offered something that seemed full of promise but was just another deal.

Which only prompted me to my life. The shit show that it was.

I could take my life back now that Macon was dead, but the weight of the past was hard to lose. I felt… scarred.

"Our deal. I've made enough of them just like this. The only one who gets fucked is me."

"Literally or figuratively?"

I cut through the house, aimed for the back steps off the kitchen, then realized the last place I wanted to be with Jed was my bedroom, so I slipped into where I knew was going to be somewhat soundproofed for our argument.

"What the fuck is this?" Jed asked, following me, looking around.

"The telephone room," I replied. It was a tiny space beneath the back stairs meant for one. "My great-grandfather built this place. Back in his day, it was added when he got a telephone. It was the only one in the house, so it was a space for privacy."

Jed reached his arms out and easily touched two of

the walls. There was a small nook in the wall where the phone went and a corner bench seat. The walls were painted a deep burgundy and the single brass light fixture made the space oddly cozy instead of claustrophobic.

It was Jed though, that made it feel that way. He took up most of the space. Reaching back, he grabbed the door and pulled it shut behind us.

The shotgun went off again, but I barely heard it this time.

Maybe coming in here was a stupid choice. The only exit was behind him.

"What did Macon do to you?"

"Get out, Jed," I said on a sigh. I'd been up since five to exercise. In the office by seven-thirty. I'd left early today because of dinner with my brothers, but I wouldn't have gotten home until close to nine. Normally.

Work filled my time. My thoughts. It kept me moving and moving was good, because if I slowed down, I thought. If I thought, I turned into this. A barely drunk thirty-year-old with no life. Hardly any friends. Nothing but... fuck me. Unhappiness.

The last thing I wanted to do was talk about Macon.

"No."

I stared at his lips as he uttered that one word. The scent of him filled the room. Pheromones and clean male. Laundry soap.

"There's not enough room for both of us."

"Then why did you come in here? It's not like you could hide from me."

I closed my eyes. Sighed. Felt the liquor bottle pulled from my fingers.

"What did Macon do to you?" he asked again.

"Do?"

"Did he hit you? Is that how he controlled you?" Fury filled his gaze as he raked it over me, looking for signs of Macon's anger on my body.

"He never touched me," I admitted.

"What other deals have you made with Macon? Other people? Who... who—" When he couldn't finish his question, I looked up at him. Leaned back at his intensity. Anger was pumping off him in waves. His jaw was clenched, his eyes fierce. Every line of his body was taut as if exposed to a live wire. "Who did he make you fuck?"

No one had ever, *ever,* asked me that. How he even got to that question made me realize he could see all too much.

"What do you mean?"

"You accused me of it at the wake."

My throat clogged up with tears, but I willed them away. I didn't cry. It was weakness that could be used against me. Even with Jed. Emotions were powerful weapons.

I raised a hand between us, set it on his chest. I could feel the steady thump of his heart beneath my palm. "Stop."

He ran his fingers over his beard. "Stop? Are you serious? Your father... Jesus, he *used* you."

"I never said that," I countered.

"You didn't have to. It's obvious to me. While you might have a pretty good poker face, you can't hide from me."

I shrugged, tipped up my chin and gave him a practiced smile. Hiding everything.

He waited, then ripped off his hat and set it in the nook where the phone used to be. He set the whiskey bottle on the bench seat. "Now I know why you're the ice princess."

The smile slipped. Barely. Then he grabbed my upper arms.

"He's put you through hell, hasn't he? You hide to protect yourself, but I see you."

I widened my eyes in surprise, not that he was dangerous, but that this close, I saw how pissed he was. The fire in his eyes. I could *feel* it. It was *for* me.

He'd asked me to trust him. I couldn't. He'd also offered his touch and I craved that. Not just the orgasms he gave me, but the connection. Needed someone right now. I was tired of being alone.

"Come on, princess. Melt for me."

Melt for him.

Yes. I took what I wanted in this moment. I could take what he offered, but on my terms. I pushed up on my tiptoes and kissed him. Hooked my hand around his neck. For a second, he didn't move, didn't respond, and then he was kissing me back. Rough. Wild. Our mouths opened, tongues tangled. I felt the soft rasp of his beard. Heads tilted to get even closer. His arms went around my back and lifted me up. My legs went around his waist, forcing the hem of my dress to slide up my thighs.

He took one step and pressed me into the wall.

His hands ran over me, cupping my breast, sliding down my hip, along my thigh. My dress went up and I felt it all. I'd never been so hot for someone before. So... desperate.

The escorts I fucked were skilled, knew exactly what they were doing. While I couldn't say they'd faked it—their hard dicks couldn't lie—it was only arousal. The need to orgasm that drove them. Also, the money.

They'd learned I couldn't come with them. Took it as perhaps a female defect and let it go. They hadn't understood like Jed had because their fragile egos wouldn't have been able to handle it. Jed had handled it. Didn't think it was a big deal. Didn't think I was broken. Maybe wired differently, but he'd gotten me there just the same. Let me help.

I wanted more of it. This? With Jed? It was lust. Passion. Need. It was hot and intense and crazy.

Stupid, probably. He'd said he'd showed up at the wake to pay his respects. As an employee of John Marshall. But had he told the truth when he said he saw me and wanted me? The probing questions he'd been asking made me think so.

The thick prod of his dick against my belly made it seem legit too, but was that all he wanted? Could I have been safe from everyone else, and then the one person who fed me lines I wanted to hear was getting past all my walls?

All I knew was that I wanted him. I loved how he made me feel. How... pretty I felt when he looked at me. How safe. Protected. How *hot.*

Yeah, I wanted this. The connection. The release. If there were consequences, I'd expect them and deal with them later.

"That's right, you'll melt for me," he practically

growled when he cupped me, discovering that I was still bare since I gave him my panties at my office.

"This is just another business deal," I panted, loving the feel of his beard against my skin.

He reared back, his hand stilled. His chest heaved as if he'd run a marathon and his hair was tousled. His lips were slick and red. Yet his fingers slid over my folds, gently, spreading my wetness around. He was petting me, caressing, watching. Working me up.

"No *business* deal, princess. I said I'd get you to trust me. I'm not here to fuck you over. I don't have an agenda. This is different."

He rolled his hips and his dick rocked against my clit. I whimpered.

"I saw you. That was it."

"Love at first sight?" I asked with a huff of a laugh because it was totally unbelievable.

He shrugged one broad shoulder. "Something like that. This isn't business. No Marshall. No Macon. It's very, *very* personal. Just between you and me. No one else."

My eyes fell closed because his touch felt so good.

His lips brushed over mine and I sank into it. He licked into me, claimed my mouth as he slid a finger into me. My back arched as he slowly fucked me with it, then added another.

I was writhing my hips, eager for more. My fingers clung to his shoulders.

"Jed!" I cried. I was so worked up, I was lost to him. His fingers rubbed over a spot and it was like a magic button. I groaned.

"There, huh?"

I didn't reply because it was so good. I wasn't going to come, but I was closer than I ever had been with anyone else. And it was only his fingers.

He stilled, slipped them from me. When I blinked my lids open, he was hovering over me. So close. "It's you and me. For once, trust."

I nodded because I could only feel. Then he licked his fingers.

The action, knowing he was tasting me, that I was so wet that it was all over him, was dirty. That he saw me this way, sexual. Perhaps passionate. Desirable.

I reached between us, worked on his belt. Since my thighs were clamped around his waist, he was able to use both hands, grab a condom from his pocket then push his jeans down. I heard the sound of foil, then the bump of Jed's hands as he slid on protection, then set himself right at my entrance. My pussy clenched in anticipation.

His eyes met mine. Held.

"Do it," I said, then my breath was cut off as he thrust up hard, filling me in one stroke.

"Fuck," he growled, his head settling at my neck.

A hand went to my ass and squeezed as my body rippled and stretched to accommodate him. I hadn't seen how big he was, but I felt it.

The tiny room was warm. Sweat dotted my skin. My dress was bunched and probably wrinkled. And I was aching and throbbing with need.

He rolled his hips, pulled back and thrust. Again and again.

We didn't say anything. Didn't need to. I clung and grabbed, rolled my hips and bowed my back. Got worked and fucked and filled.

"North."

I blinked my eyes open at my name. His face was right there, his gaze heavy lidded and dark. Wild and untamed.

He took one of my hands from his hair and brought it between us, set his fingers over mine on my clit. "Show me how."

I stared at him, confused, then he moved his fingers, moving mine. He wanted me to come. Knew this was how to do it.

I took over, adjusting my fingers in the flat way I liked, made the usual small circles.

He thrust deep and I moved faster. God, the thick feel of him and having my clit worked. It was...

"Oh," I whispered.

"Good girl. You're going to come for me." He talked as he rocked his hips, slowly fucking me. "You feel so good. Fuck, so tight. So wet."

Then he got filthier. Both hands cupped my bare ass, but a finger slipped between and over my back entrance and—

I clamped down on his dick and came. "Holy shit!" I cried, my fingers still strumming my clit as a fingertip brushed over me *there.*

White lights danced behind my closed eyelids. My fingers tingled, my body was wracked with the most amazing pleasure. Being filled so deep, my clit being stimulated was amazing, but it was that extra touch I had no idea would feel so good.

Sharp and bright. Hot and intense.

"Fuck, you're strangling my dick." Jed had been holding back but no longer, fucking me through my orgasm with uncontrolled thrusts. He growled, then held himself deep, his mouth sucking at my neck as he pulsed inside of me.

The telephone room was like a little sauna. All I could hear was our ragged breathing. I hadn't noticed any more shots fired, although if the house blew up, I probably wouldn't have known.

Because in this little nook beneath the stairs, the world slipped away. Nothing existed but me and Jed. Of how he made me feel.

There was no North, the CEO. No North, Macon's daughter. No North, the older sister. I was just... princess.

For once in my life, I was okay with that. Because I'd done the one thing I never thought I could do. Let down my guard. Let someone in. Trust. And it felt so, so good.

But it never lasted. I had to wonder how it was going to blow up in my face, because eventually everything good did.

7

JED

NORTH WAS IN THE SHOWER. Her dog had been laying outside the telephone room door while I'd taken her. He'd followed her upstairs. I wanted to join her, but we'd never get out. I'd take her there, press her up against the tile, or if it had a bench seat bend her over it. Fuck yes. Then I'd carry her to her bed, or nearest horizontal surface, and take her again.

That was why I was in the kitchen trying to figure out food while imagining her naked and wet, soap suds sliding over her perfect tits and toned thighs.

I was hard. It had been ten minutes since I'd had

the hardest, most intense orgasm of my life. It hadn't scratched the itch. Hell, it made it ten times worse. I didn't think she was ready for more. Not yet. Physically, sure. Her pussy was wet and aching for sex, but mentally? She might be the most poised and focused person I've ever met, but she was also ridiculously vulnerable. Yeah, I saw it, even when she didn't want me to.

Getting her to trust me when she didn't trust anyone...

I needed patience. And so did my dick.

My cell vibrated in my pocket. I pulled it out, read the display. My boss. I had to answer it. I'd put her off.

"Yeah," I said.

"Any update on the order?" she asked. I envisioned her in her office overlooking the thick Virginia forest that surrounded Quantico.

"I met with the supplier this morning, but the paperwork was missing. I'll check back later."

"Jed—"

"She didn't do it," I said, ensuring my boss knew how I felt, that North was innocent. "We're looking at the wrong supplier."

"You have proof?"

"No." I couldn't tell her what we'd just done, that

my case was compromised because I was falling for the suspect. She might not even care because I was the only one who could lead this case. Anyone else would stick out like a nun in a whorehouse. They were all city slickers.

"Then you know what to do."

I wasn't going to tell her I was with North now, in her house. That I'd had the best sex of my life in a vintage telephone room. My job was to find out about the deal and that was the update. I hung up and tucked my cell away. While the house was huge, I wouldn't risk being overheard. But she wouldn't be put off for long. It only made me realize how fucked up this situation was. I was hard. Even after coming so hard I'd gone blind for a few seconds, my dick hadn't gone down.

I opened the huge fridge and stared inside, hoping the cool air would help. Then I remembered how she tasted, like whiskey and sin. Remembered the clamp of her pussy when she came. The...

"The cook leaves a note."

I stuck my head around the open door at the voice.

South. He scanned the huge marble topped island, then pointed to a piece of paper propped against a vase of fresh flowers. "There. North doesn't cook and Macon sure as shit didn't. The guy's here every day prepping meals and having it ready to go whenever they get home from the office."

I was closer, so I grabbed it.

"Chicken enchiladas in the warming drawer," I read. "Guacamole and sour cream in the fridge."

Fuck, that sounded good. Unlike the Wainrights, I could cook, although my ranch kitchen was nothing like this one. A bachelor would starve without some talent with a knife and a frying pan, but I had a feeling this meal was going to be epic because Macon would have fired anyone whose food was bad.

"Want a beer?" he asked.

If he had any issues with me fucking his sister beneath the back stairs, he didn't let on. Then again, he and his brothers had been busy outside shooting up shit and I figured he had no idea. I doubted he'd offer me a beer if he had.

"Sure."

Leaning against the counter, I watched as he went around the island, bent down and opened a door. He pulled out a beer, then another from what I assumed was a small wine fridge.

He slid it across the counter to me. I took it, removed the cap and took a pull. My throat was dry from making North come hard around my dick.

"Grab one for me," East said as he came in from

the mud room, setting the bottle of whiskey on the counter. It wasn't even half empty, meaning they weren't drunk.

West followed, carrying the guns. He tipped his chin in my direction as he veered out of the room, probably to stow the weapons.

I'd seen pictures of the Wainright men in my files, but they were bigger in person. East had said he'd played football in high school and college. He'd have been big then, especially to get a scholarship for it, but he was probably even bigger now. I pegged him at six-four, two hundred twenty pounds. I'd watched him devour a sub sandwich at his father's wake and imagined he needed lots of calories to fuel his tank.

South was shorter and leaner. Had more of a runner's build, but could hold his own, I had no doubt.

West came back minus the shotguns. East had grabbed a beer for him and passed it off. They all had various shades of brown hair, but none looked much alike. None looked like North.

They were all staring at me, the center island the size of my kitchen, between us.

I had to wonder how guys this big couldn't deal with Macon and protect their sister.

"You and North, huh?" West asked, looking me over.

Three brothers could be hard to win over, but I had a feeling they might be easier than North herself.

"Me and North," I replied, not giving them anything more. I knew what I wanted from North—everything, especially after what we'd just done—but she wasn't there yet. "My condolences about your father."

They glanced at each other and laughed, took swigs of beer. "Yeah, thanks," South offered, but he didn't seem all that torn up. None of them did.

"Didn't see you at the wake," I commented, looking at South and West.

"North had it handled," West said.

"You sure about that?" I asked. Having to deal with snoopy townsfolk solo didn't seem fair. Or fun.

"We were on our way but East texted and said North shot up the place and shut the thing down. No one's going to fuck with our sister."

"Yeah, you don't know our sister," West added.

I didn't, but I was starting to. If her brothers were giving her a hard time, I'd set them straight. I didn't care that they looked like part of a national rugby team and could shoot a flea off a squirrel's back.

"Do you?" I countered.

South bristled, his shoulders rolling back, his eyes narrowing. "What the fuck's your problem? You come waltzing in here like you know what's going on around here."

"You're her brothers. It's your job to watch out for her."

"You mean hug her while she cries about our father dying?" West asked. "She won't shed a tear for him. None of us will. We're all glad to see him in the ground."

East held up a hand and his brothers quieted. "I don't think that's what he means." He glanced at his brothers who flanked him, then back at me. "What do you know that we don't? North never tells us shit. You're here and talking like someone's fucking with her."

West's back went straight. "What? Who? A visit from the three of us should get any guy to back off and shit his pants."

I agreed with that.

"I'd start with your dad," I said simply, although I was pleased to hear West was protective of North.

They went still, as if they'd been hit with a stun gun. Their jaws clenched and their eyes narrowed, but that's all.

"What did he do?" South asked finally, his voice low. Even. Too even.

I shrugged, although I had a pretty good idea. If I was correct, her brothers deserved to know. "Not sure yet. She told me someone had to follow in her father's footsteps. I'm thinking she didn't have much choice."

South looked down at the floor, swore under his breath. "That girl, so fucking stubborn. And a liar. No one *had* to take over the business. It can fold for all I care."

"Except the... what, thousand or more employees who are out of work in central Montana?" I countered.

He clenched his jaw, catching on to the extent of North's burdens. "You think he hurt her and she didn't tell us about it?"

"What is she to you?" East asked, ignoring South and homing in on me. "Heard you came to the wake for your boss."

I had no idea how he'd picked that up, but it didn't surprise me.

West raised a brow in question and East added, "John Marshall."

When they turned their gazes on me this time, it was clear they knew the kind of man Marshall was. Which meant they probably thought the same of me. Birds of a feather and all that.

"It's your job to protect North because you're her brothers," I said, leaving Marshall out of this. "It's my job to protect her because she's *mine.* If anyone's going to spank her ass for putting herself in danger, that'll be me."

After what we'd just done in that tiny room, there was no going back.

"She know that?" West asked.

"Getting there," I replied, then looked to South. "Like you said, she's stubborn."

"Marshall's an asshole. Why should we trust a guy who works for him?" South asked.

"Because I'm starting to," North said, coming into the room. Her feet were bare, so she'd been silent. If she'd had on her heels, we wouldn't have missed her approach.

Her brothers weren't going to welcome me into the family anytime soon. I didn't give a shit because I was into North, not them. I'd warm her bed and keep her safe, hear her secrets. Carry her burdens. I could do all that when they returned to their lives... elsewhere.

She wore a pair of yoga pants the color of an eggplant and a long-sleeved t-shirt that went below her perfect hips and ass. She was covered from neck to ankle but her soft curves were showcased. I was thankful for the counter to hide my hard on.

"I'm getting through Macon's deals at the office. I had Julian put the Marshall at the top of the pile and I went through it earlier." She stared at me with her shrewd blue eyes. She hadn't found anything damning, either for me or the deal, in what she'd read. No way would she have let me touch her if she had. She'd had a shotgun in her hand for the second time and I wasn't dead yet.

"And?" West asked.

North went to the warming drawer, which was directly beneath the double ovens. Taking a dishtowel that hung from the handle, she used it to lift the dish of enchiladas and set them on the butcher block.

"Marshall bought two thousand acres up near Provost. Macon's buying it from him," she said.

That was the basis of the deal. It was completely true, in two sentences.

"Why? What makes that parcel special?" South asked as North pulled plates from a cabinet. When she raised her arms to grab them, her shirt rode up and I got a good look at her ass in those snug pants. I'd had my hands on it just a little while ago and I was ready to peel them off her. With my teeth.

"Wainright Holdings purchases land seen as potentially vulnerable. We buy it to protect whatever's there, endangered wildlife or threatened forests. Some we keep, some we donate to be kept wild for future generations." She spoke as she worked collecting napkins and silverware, not looking at any of her brothers. It sounded like she was giving her brothers a sales pitch.

"That doesn't sound like Macon," West scoffed.

"Yeah," South agreed, grabbing a spatula from a crock by the stove and began scooping enchiladas onto plates, forcing North to move out of the way.

"It sounds like me," she said.

Her brothers turned to her.

She shrugged. "It's what I handle at the office. It's what's important to me. What was important to Mom."

For perhaps the first time—except when I'd been inside her—I heard softness in North's voice. *This* was her passion, what she was meant to do. I'd known about her role as head of philanthropy, but never heard her speak of it. How she felt about it. This was the real North talking to her brothers. I got to see it and it made me question if she knew what was planned for that land next. I'd swear she had no idea, not in her bare feet and holding a plate of enchiladas.

But my boss wouldn't take that as evidence. If the land deal went through, it only made her more of a suspect. Since Marshall hadn't called me, I figured it hadn't.

"Macon didn't give a shit about Mom," East said, taking a filled plate from South. He'd been two or three when she'd died and I doubt he remembered the woman, but I was sure Macon had shared his feelings.

South looked to me, tipped his head toward the fridge. "Grab the guac and sour cream."

I retrieved them, then set the toppings beside the tray. East immediately scooped guac and put it on top of his food, like whipped cream on a sundae.

"That's why I work there. I've kept Macon in line all this time and now that I'm CEO, I can steer the company where Mom always wanted it to go," she said. It was the same thing she told me.

"You've kept Macon in line?" South asked, setting a filled plate on the counter in front of North.

North stilled as she reached for the sour cream, looked up at her brother. "Yeah, I have."

She hadn't kept Macon from all his shady business dealings. She either knew about them, and let them slide. Or she'd been kept in the dark and she was referencing something else entirely.

"Is that why you stayed in this house? Worked with him day in and day out? To keep him in line?" West asked around a mouthful of Mexican food.

It was impressive the way North put on a shield of protection like anyone else would a coat. Her brothers didn't seem to notice, but the ice princess was back. West's question had her walls going up. I'd been right in my thinking. She'd made some kind of deal... or deals with her father to protect her brothers. He might not have beaten her or touched her inappropriately, but he'd used her nonetheless. She'd sold herself for her brothers' happiness.

"I didn't do a very good job, did I?" she asked, her voice soft but laced with steel.

East looked to me, as if our little chat before she'd come downstairs had been an awakening for him. "What did he do to you?"

"Nothing," she replied, stabbing her enchilada with a fork.

East dropped his plate onto the counter with a clatter. North startled.

He rested his palms on the marble, leaned in and glared at her. "We're your brothers. Tell us what he fucking did."

A flush crept up North's cheeks, but she stayed silent.

East tossed up his hands in frustration. "Fuck, North. Do I look like I can't handle Macon?" He glanced at South and West. "That they can't either?"

"You have no idea," she whispered.

"Then tell us!" he shouted.

She jumped. Her hand shook and she set her fork down.

I grabbed her, pulled her into my arms, her back to my front. Since she was barefoot, I was able to set my chin on the top of her head. It was the closest I could come to wrapping her up, holding her as close to me as I could.

I wanted to tell East to lay off, but it was clear he had no clue what had been going on. He'd earned his anger because I felt the same fury at Macon Wainright, and I wasn't even Macon's kid. I hadn't grown up in this house.

But North needed comfort, to know she was safe as her brothers raged. That whatever happened hadn't been her fault. Tipping my head down, I murmured in her ear. "Tell them, princess. What you did for them."

I wasn't sure of my words, but I said them anyway. A bluff. To get her to think I knew, that it wasn't a secret any longer. She was safe with me. With her brothers.

No one talked. No one moved. The guys waited. I held my breath, hoped she finally, *finally* unburden.

"I let you go to college," she said, her voice soft, as if it was hard to get out.

"What do you mean *let you*?" South asked. His plate was untouched on the counter.

She looked up, met her brothers' gazes across the kitchen island. "Macon wasn't going to let you go. Any of you."

"Why?" East asked, frowning.

"Because he was an asshole," she said. She was shaking and I held her even closer.

"You went," East stated.

She nodded. "Yeah, to the school he wanted. The major he wanted."

"It was South's turn the next year. What did you do?" East added.

"I made a deal. Deals."

She exhaled. I felt the secret literally deflate her.

I'd been right and I'd been angry in my thoughts. But she validated them, and it made it all so much worse.

"You made a deal with Macon so I could go to college?" South asked. "I was eighteen. I could have just left. Walked away from it all."

I shifted slightly so I could see North's profile, watched as she licked her lips. "You wanted to go to art school. You know how he thought about that. He was going to destroy you. Somehow."

South's eyes widened. "How the fuck was he going to do that?"

"I don't know. He didn't say. Whatever it took to push you away from it." The words came easier for her now.

"And me?" East asked. "He got me kicked off the football team and I almost lost my scholarship. You got him to change his mind?"

She nodded. "He was going to have your leg broken so you couldn't get the scholarship."

East spun on his heel, walked away.

Holy fuck. The man was going to have his kid's leg broken?

"And me?" West asked, his teeth clenched.

"Does it matter?"

West's nostrils flared. "To me it does! So we got college and what did he get in return?" West asked.

North shook her head and she was almost brittle in my arms. "I can't tell you that. You know the truth and that's enough. I did what I had to do to get you out of here. To protect you. To make your dreams come true."

"What about your dreams?" South asked. Now he wasn't angry but devastated.

I loosened my hold when she tried to turn. She faced me, set her forehead on my chest. I sighed, pleased that she sought comfort from me, from my arms around her.

Fuck me, this woman. She was killing me.

I didn't know all of it, like what she'd bargained away. I had a feeling she'd done a hell of a lot more of it than just for her brothers. Like with Jock, too.

This was a start. I bent down so we were eye to eye. "You did good."

"I'm… I'm not hungry," she murmured. The fire was gone from her eyes. No ice either. Just… weariness. "I'm going to go to bed. See you around."

See you around? Fuck that.

I kissed her forehead, then released her. She headed out of the kitchen, but South went around the island to stop her. He tugged her into his arms, gave her a fierce hug. East and West joined him, one stroking her head, the other taking her hand. Then they let her go.

They didn't say anything for a bit, perhaps to let North work her way through the big house. West grabbed the whiskey bottle and fiercely unscrewed the lid. Took a huge swallow.

"She turned to you," he said.

I nodded. "I may have shown up at the wake for Marshall, but I'm here for North."

"Get the truth from her," West ordered. Obviously,

he'd seen the way she turned to me. "If there's anyone alive who was involved in these deals, I want to know. We're ending them."

South and East nodded, flanking their brother. They were united now, not just in hatred for Macon, but as protectors of North.

I didn't even give a shit they just told an FBI agent they were considering premeditated murder. Because I might be the one to give them the bullets.

8

NORTH

I FLOPPED down on my bed and stared up at the ceiling. Maybe it had been the whiskey that had gotten the secrets out of me. Maybe it was the orgasm in the telephone room. I could still feel the throb of Jed being inside me. The soreness of being taken so hard, so thoroughly.

The emotions bombarding me were too much. Amazing sex. Sex where there was an actual connection, where it had been too hot, too intense I'd lost my mind. I'd screamed when I came. Thank God for sturdy, vintage house construction.

It had been the best sex of my life, with a guy who

drove me crazy. He was as bossy as me. Worse, because he got his way. That wasn't the reason why I wanted to climb him like a tree and shoot him at the same time. It was because I *liked* it when he told me what to do.

That was scary as shit because Macon had ordered me around and I'd had to give in. There'd been no winning with him. Compromise, perhaps. Maybe in-the-moment success, but in the long run, I'd always lost.

Why was I falling for Jed? Did I have a Daddy complex? I groaned because that was just ridiculous and a completely scary thought. I flopped over onto my stomach.

It didn't matter. Jed was probably halfway back to his place by now. He'd gotten what he'd wanted. In my pants. Well, beneath my dress. He'd gotten off and I'd trusted him while he'd done it.

The end.

I rolled over, stared at the ceiling some more.

I'd have to face my brothers again. Eventually. They had even more reason to hate their father. It didn't matter because he was dead. It was over. Macon's hold over all of us was over.

Was it though? I'd looked through the files Julian had collected for me. After Jed left this morning, I'd spent my time between meetings reading through what my father had been up to. Outstanding deals Macon had been working on. Some I'd known about; others were new to me.

I'd pored over his deal with Marshall. The original owner of the land wouldn't sell to Macon, probably because he'd burned a bridge with the man. But he'd sold to Marshall. Macon was going to buy it from him. I was now expected to buy it from Marshall, which was why Jed had come around in the first place.

Marshall was out millions on a piece of land he probably didn't even want. He'd turn a nice profit based on what Macon had agreed to pay him to be the middleman. Marshall never expected Macon to up and die. Since the deal wasn't with Macon personally but with Wainright Holdings, someone had to sign on the dotted line. And hand over the cash.

Jed had said he'd gone to the wake for Marshall, then stayed for me. His appearance at my office this morning had been part of his job. Was that why he'd shown up here tonight? To give me orgasms in trade for finishing what Macon had promised?

Was I only a transaction to Jed? There was one way to find out. I climbed from the bed, pulled my laptop from my leather satchel and sat down at my desk. It faced west and the view was impressive. The sun was setting, and I watched as it slowly slipped behind the craggy peaks. I pulled up the legal paperwork for Marshall's deal on my laptop, signed it at the indicated places, hit the submit button.

It was done.

The contract for the land was signed. I grabbed my cell from the slim pocket in my leggings, called Julian. He answered on the first ring, as usual, no matter the time of day.

"The land contract with Marshall is signed," I told him. "Ensure the wire for the funds goes through during banking hours tomorrow."

"On it," he replied, then hung up.

I watched as the color of the sky changed from orange to pink. I loved it here. The land. The house. Everything that my family had built for generations. It didn't make any sense since Macon had tainted it all.

My brothers. Me.

Especially me.

I felt a nudge at my calf and I looked down. Eddie. I petted him and his tail bumped against the leg of my desk as it went back and forth. I hadn't closed the door all the way and he'd nudged it open to settle into the dog bed in the corner where he slept at night.

He followed me everywhere around the house. Sometimes I took him to the office when I drove, but most of the time since I took the helicopter, he remained here and slept. Since he wasn't a puppy any longer, that was what he did all day. Plus snore and fart.

Macon had complained about how horrible a guard dog he was.

I hadn't gotten Eddie to protect me. The dog gave me unconditional love and wanted nothing in return. As I stared down at that sweet face and thought about it, it was really fucking sad.

"Every guy wants a little attention from you."

I whipped my head around and my heart skipped a beat. Jed was in my doorway, filling most of it. He took off his hat, tossed it onto my reading chair in the corner. It was beside a fireplace, now cold.

"How did you find your way up here?" I asked.

He pointed to the dog. "He follows you everywhere."

"So do you," I replied. I'd never been more vulnerable than when with Jed. Even Macon didn't make me feel this way. I'd hidden my emotions well from my father, or he hadn't wanted to really see them.

But Jed *saw* me. I had no idea how. Or why he'd want someone as fucked up as me.

I stood and Eddie loped over to his bed. "Why did you do that, in the kitchen?"

"What?"

I crossed my arms over my chest. "Make me tell my brothers. It wasn't your secret to tell."

"You're right, it was yours. They deserve to know, North. What their father did. What he was really like."

I laughed. "They knew."

He shook his head. "They had no idea."

I threw my hands up in the air because he knew how to drive me crazy. Drive me wild. He infuriated me and intrigued me. When he came running around the house because he'd heard shots, a thrill had gone through me. To see the concern on his face.

He'd run toward gun shots for me.

Which only circled my thoughts back to what he wanted. Why would he run toward danger for a woman he hardly knew? Why was he still here, really? He'd already gotten sex and yet he was still around after that shit show in the kitchen. He wasn't done with his mission.

Was he here for the deal? He didn't know I'd signed the papers. Only Julian did. He'd fucked me and in the morning, he'd learn the deal was done.

Did I enjoy him tonight before he moved on? Marshall would have his money and Jed would be redirected to someone else to work over. I'd gained a nice parcel of land and a few steamy memories. I'd never be able to go into the telephone room again without thinking of wallbanging sex and Jed.

"Am I different?" I asked.

He came in the room, closed the door behind him.

"Different?" he repeated.

I stood from the desk, closed the lid on the laptop. The sky was now purple, bleeding toward black.

"You work for Marshall."

"Yes." He undid the cuff on one of his shirtsleeves.

"He sent you to the wake."

"Yes." He undid the other.

"Do you fuck men who have deals that need closing?"

He tugged the tails of his shirt from his jeans. "I like being the only one with a beard in a relationship."

He didn't seem bothered by my probing questions, which pissed me off. Why was he so… relaxed all the time?

"What are you doing?" I asked. While I was enjoying the show of him stripping out of his shirt—and the broad expanse of chest and six-pack abs—I didn't know why he was taking his clothes off.

"Getting ready for bed."

My mouth fell open as he tossed the shirt onto my chair beside his hat. I hadn't wanted him in this space, having this room filled with memories of him.

"Here?"

"Here."

"I don't want you in my bedroom."

"You told me that before. Too intimate?"

I blinked as he undid his belt buckle.

"Y-yes."

He dropped his hands, the belt laying open at his waist. God, he was gorgeous. The dark hair, olive skin, the dense muscles. His calm demeanor drove me bonkers. Why didn't he get riled? Throw things? Shout? That I could handle. But that strong jaw and beard, the way he skillfully used his fingers were things I didn't know how to deal with.

He frazzled my brain cells.

"What we did in that tiny room downstairs wasn't intimate?"

It had been. Shit, he was right.

"Take off your clothes, princess."

He got back to work on his. I couldn't do anything but watch because… wow.

Soon he was naked before me. N.A.K.E.D.

Every encounter we'd had so far he hadn't taken off his clothes. Only his pants had been opened earlier. Nothing more and I hadn't even gotten a glimpse. Now he stood before me as an amazing specimen of man. Perfectly proportioned, better than

David, and dappled in dark hair. And that dick. My pussy clenched. That had been in me?

It was long and thick, perfectly formed. It bobbed, angled up and toward me. I could see pre-cum beading at the tip of the flared crown. I hadn't watched a lot of porn, but he had a fallback career with that thing.

"Don't make me say it again," he said, cutting through my staring, and drooling.

My nipples beaded beneath my t-shirt so I crossed my arms.

"Don't tell me what to do," I snapped.

"Keep talking to me in that tone and we'll see what else you can do with that mouth," he countered.

My mouth fell open and I snapped it shut. I couldn't believe we were having this conversation with him bare assed. Of course he wasn't the least bit modest standing in the middle of my bedroom.

I laughed to hide how his words turned me on. I glanced down at his dick, imagining it stretching my mouth wide as he'd insinuated.

"I won't kneel for you," I countered, straightening my shoulders.

He took a step toward me. His dick swayed. I swallowed.

"I'll be the *only* one you kneel for," he said, his eyes

narrowing. He came close, close enough to stroke my hair back, for his dick to press into my belly. "You like when I take control."

I shook my head, but his hand slipped around and wrapped in my hair. Tugged.

The slight bite of pain had me gasping. I met his eyes as he held me in place.

"Out there," he tipped his head indicating anywhere outside this room. "You're in charge. You can juggle all the fucking balls you want. Make the deals in those dresses and high heels. That dressy armor you wear. In here, when you're wet and aching for some attention, I am."

Was that what drew me to him, the fact that when we were alone, I didn't have to do anything but be me? To feel something real? I wanted that. As much as I craved to lick off that drop of pre-cum and taste him on my tongue.

I stepped back, wrapped my arms tighter around myself. "How do I know if this is real?"

"I'm standing here buck naked, princess. I've got nothing to hide."

I couldn't look at him, at every inch of tanned skin and sinewy muscle, so I closed my eyes.

I heard him sigh. "He destroyed you."

"Yeah, he did," I admitted, knowing he was talking

about Macon. "I've got a hot guy, naked and hard and we're *talking.* Any whole woman would be riding your dick now."

"He's six feet under, princess. You're here. It's time to pick up the pieces and make the life you want."

"That's what you want to do, pick up all the pieces of me? Am I even worth it?"

I heard something like a growl come out of him before I was scooped up in the air and tossed onto the bed. Instinctively, I popped up onto my hands and knees facing the headboard to move away from him, but he grabbed my ankle.

Glaring over my shoulder, I met his dark stare. I was breathing hard. "What are you doing?"

"Getting answers," he replied. His grip remained on my ankle as his other hand came down on my upturned ass in a hard spank.

"Jed!" I shouted as I tried to kick him with my free leg.

He yanked me back, which had me dropping to my stomach on the soft mattress. He shifted, tugged me onto his lap so my toes touched the carpet while my torso was still on the bed. "What did I say about talking bad about yourself?"

He spanked me again, then tugged down my yoga

pants. Another growl. "Good girl. You're learning how I like you. Without panties."

Another spank, this time on my bare ass.

He wasn't gentle and it hurt, but the sting morphed into heat. And I was angry, so I had that fueling me. Yet his dirty talk made me hot and that made me wonder who I was mad at. Him or myself. Either way, I said, "I hate you."

"In your deals with Macon to get your brothers to college, what did you offer?"

I squirmed, which only had me feeling every inch of how hard he was.

"We finished this downstairs," I replied.

"Not even close, princess. Let's start with South. He was a year after you in school. What did you give your father for South's freedom?"

I gripped the bedding and stayed silent. He waited a second, then another, then began to spank me. Hard. One cheek then the other. "Jed!" I shouted, but he didn't stop.

I saw Eddie on his bed, curled up and sound asleep. I wasn't getting any help from him.

Jed was relentless.

The pain got to be too much and I had no idea if Jed would ever stop. "I switched majors!"

His hand settled on my hot skin. "Keep going."

I was sweating and angry and turned on, which made me angrier.

"I wanted to study forestry," I said. "To be a park ranger. But Macon wanted me in business, to take over. Said I couldn't do that or get my MBA if I was fucking Smoky Bear."

I loved the land. The wilderness. Jed didn't know that it was my only escape. Hiking or horseback riding. Snowmobiling. I owned enough of it that I had it all to myself. Except every acre that belonged to me was only that, an escape. It wasn't my life.

"So Daddy picked your major in trade for South to be an artist. What about East?"

I didn't say anything, remembering back to that conversation all those years ago.

"Need a little refresher of who's in charge here?" Jed asked. "You talk or I spank."

I huffed, then turned my head. I was in an awkward position over his lap but fighting seemed useless.

"After my sophomore year, I came home from Harvard for the summer instead of working on the Cape like my friends. He put me in the mail room. I worked sixty hours a week in the basement of Wainright Holdings. Starting at the bottom."

"Nothing wrong with the mail room," he said, knowing there was more to this than just hard work.

"You're right," I replied. "I met the nicest people. Genuine, unlike Macon and his cronies."

"You said Macon threatened to break East's leg. He wasn't doing it to fuck with your brother, he was doing it to get something from you."

I groaned, then pushed up. He let me but took my leggings off as I moved. My t-shirt was long enough to cover my ass, but that wasn't why I felt exposed. Tucking my legs under me, I sat in the middle of my bed as Jed, naked, remained on the side.

"Macon rewarded me by pulling me out of the basement. Dinner meetings to learn the ropes." I made finger quotes in the air for the last. "Turns out, I wasn't the only one he made deals with. In fact, for East, I was the offering."

He stood, grabbed his jeans from the floor and tugged them on. He didn't button them, but when he turned to face me and he raked his hand through his hair, he was at least covered.

"He offered you how?" he asked. "Golf partner?"

I laughed. "I'm actually pretty good at golf. But no. I was to fuck a potential business connection."

Jed went over to the fireplace, grabbed a glass vase and threw it into the cold hearth. It shattered into pieces, some flying across the carpet. Eddie lifted his head but settled back to sleep when I didn't move.

"Did you?" he asked finally, running a hand over his beard.

"I knew in advance. He told me what I was going to do for him. Giving my consent was the trade for East staying healthy and going off to school like his brothers. The night it was to happen, I told him I had my period. To stall. Fortunately, that worked. It seemed Macon didn't want to even hear about such things." It had disgusted him. "He pushed it back a week, but that was when he had East kicked off the team, putting extra pressure on me. I had to go through with it or he'd have lost his scholarship, and broken his leg."

I licked my lips. I hadn't told anyone about this. It was hard because while it had been consent, it had been coercion. Jed's anger made it easier.

"I went with Macon to the restaurant in a hotel in Billings. Made introductions. Had a drink with the guy, then Macon left. The guy, a big Texas oilman, took me up to his room. He'd had a lot to drink by then and I offered him more. It seems an overweight, sixty-year-old man with a liberal dosing of GHB in his whiskey can't get it up. Or stay conscious. Or remember anything that had happened."

"You date rape drugged him?" He didn't seem mad, more surprised. His eyebrows were at his hairline.

I shrugged, picked at the blanket. "It wasn't as if the guy was going to admit to blacking out and not remembering a fuck with North Wainright. He passed out. I left. I didn't say a word to my father and neither did the guy. The deal went through. East went to college on scholarship."

Jed strode across the room, sat on the bed again. This time, when he tugged me into his arms, he settled me on his lap so I straddled his hips. My knees were on the bed, my ass on his hard thighs. My shirt rode up and he cupped my bare butt, which was hot and sore from the spanking.

"He used you on my parents' deal. With Jock." It wasn't a question.

My mouth opened and I stared into his dark eyes. He was so close I couldn't look away. All I could see was him. The various colors in his beard. The fullness of his lips. The dark lashes women would kill for.

I stared at his lips, not because I wanted to kiss him—although I did—but because I couldn't hold his eyes for this. All I could do was nod.

"You were seventeen," he bit out.

I nodded again. I pushed back and he let me get

up. He didn't grab me or keep me from walking away. Maybe it was because I was only wearing a t-shirt that I pushed down to mid-thigh that he figured I wouldn't run. I began to pace. "He... he told me he was waiting for me to be legal, but the opportunity was too good. And because the guy he wanted me to fuck was also seventeen, it made it okay."

Out of the corner of his eye, I saw him hop to his feet and stride to me. He scooped me up. "Careful of the broken glass." His hands went to my butt, and I put my legs around his waist as he carried me this way back to the bed. I was once again straddling his lap.

"My parents were ready to sell. Why sweeten the deal?" he asked, returning to the topic.

"He wanted it to be a sure thing. Your land probably has oil. A lot of it. Macon wanted it and the best way to ensure your parents would sell to him was to make the Barnetts and the Wainrights have a connection."

"You and Jock in a relationship," he said, putting two and two together. "Don't tell me he expected you to marry him or something."

"No. Then I'd be away from him and he had lots of plans for me. With Jock, he wanted me to hand over my virginity. 'Get Jock's dick happy,' he'd said. 'Keep it that way.'" I blinked. "I remember it vividly because I was so stunned. It was the first time I'd seen the real Macon."

"You didn't do it. You broke up with him instead."

I nodded. "Jock was so sweet. I really liked him, and I couldn't have him caught up in Macon's... meanness. No one would have believed that North Wainright had a shitty father. That her life was a nightmare. Not with a house like this, not with *Billionaire Ranch*. I did the one thing I could. I told your dad he should stay away from mine, that whatever he was offering, he didn't want. Then I left."

"You destroyed his deal."

I nodded.

"What did Macon do?"

I didn't respond, so he lifted my chin so I had to look in his eyes. "What did he do?"

"This talk... we did it out of order. Jock was first. He couldn't do anything about the deal with your parents falling through. He learned something then, that there were no consequences if I stepped out of line. Nothing happened. I went to Harvard while he bided his time. Until the following year and South. Then East and West."

"Why didn't you leave after that? Your brothers

were gone. Never came back. You could've. You had your degrees. You could have gotten a job anywhere."

We could talk all night about all the ways Macon had controlled me. This was enough. He knew now why I didn't trust. Why I'd accused him of wanting something from me.

I cupped his jaw, felt the softness of his beard under my palm. "So many little cuts, Jed. They barely bleed. But they hurt just the same."

"I don't know what the fuck that means."

"It means he cut me to pieces. Only the jaded, cold parts of me are left. I'm the ice princess, remember?"

His eyes flared because he remembered his words.

"It means I have to wonder why you're here with me," I continued. "What your motive is. Your plan. What you're going to take from me."

He reached for the hem of my shirt and lifted it, slowly baring me to him. Then he shifted his knees so I slipped off. He carefully lowered me to the carpeted floor so I was kneeling before him.

"I'm not taking, princess," he said. "You're giving. Willingly and because you want to. Because beneath all the shit that's happened to you, you can tell a good thing. Something real."

"The ice princess and the fallen FBI man."

The corner of his mouth tipped up. "You read up on me."

I nodded, looking up at him. For some reason, being on the floor in front of him was... comforting. "What did you do?"

"It didn't say?" he asked.

"No."

"I made deals with the bad guys. Do you believe that, princess? You, more than anyone else, should know that not everything you read is the truth."

"You want me to trust, but—" I'd given up my life for a guy rotten to the core. Was I falling for another?

"What's your gut tell you? You're an expert on assholes. Think I'm like all the others?"

Did I? I ached for him to be better than other men. The best. But what I'd read, the fact that he worked for Marshall...

And yet I'd let him touch me within minutes at the wake. I'd let him inside me earlier. I was on my knees. *Now* I was questioning?

"You and me, we can be broken together. Two pieces put together to make a whole."

He stroked my hair as I processed what he was saying.

"You're it, princess. I'm here for you. Trust."

I shook my head, because I desperately wanted to believe his words.

"You're on your knees, but you can get up right now. Kick me out. I'll go. But I know me taking charge makes you hot."

"Jed," I breathed. He was right in that. I loved it. Needed it. Craved the blank mind. The pleasure.

He adjusted himself and the thick crown of his dick appeared in the open fly of his jeans, as if it couldn't be contained.

I wasn't the only one that craved.

"What makes you hot makes me hard. You're my woman. Whatever you desire is mine to give."

"I'm not your woman," I said right away, although hearing him say that was like a balm to an open wound. I wanted to believe him, to belong to someone. But I barely knew him, knew the bad things he'd done to be kicked out of the FBI. Did I replace one demanding man with another trying to rule my life?

"You are. The second I saw you again you were mine. When you handed me those panties in your father's office at the house surrounded by all those fucking animal heads, you gave yourself to me."

I stared up at him, leaned into his palm. The eyes were dark, fueled by all the secrets I unburdened. By the truth he seemed to be trying to get across to me over and over. He was so rugged and fierce, that calm intensity the opposite of Macon's wild rages. He showed me that he could remain in control no matter what happened, that I didn't have to fear him. Or this between us.

"It's time to make your choice, North. Either stand up and kick me out or suck my dick like a good girl."

9

JED

I WAS A FUCKING HYPOCRITE. I sat on North's bed with my dick hanging out, the woman bare and on her knees before me. I was asking her to trust, to believe that I wouldn't hurt her, wouldn't be an asshole like her father and all the mean shit he'd pushed on her.

Macon may have been devious and ruthless, using his own daughter as a pawn, but she knew what he was. She remembered me from all those years ago, but that was it. Taking the time today to research me meant she was interested and wanted to be informed. To know the full picture before going deeper with me.

Yet it was all lies. She thought I was a fallen FBI agent. Disgraced. Down on my luck and working for Marshall to pay the bills. She thought all that and was right here with me. I'd told her not everything she read was the truth. It was all I could give her, the only clue that I wasn't what she thought.

I hadn't lied, but I sure as shit hadn't told her the truth.

I couldn't.

We were the same, she and I. I was taking her innocence on faith, and she was doing the same with mine. Except I wasn't innocent. I wasn't what she thought.

I was investigating *her.* She *would* learn the truth about me, that she was my job, thinking I didn't trust her to be innocent.

I believed in her innocence, and I'd told my boss that. She didn't work in gray areas. The FBI was black and white, meaning no evidence that proved North's innocence meant she was as good as guilty.

North wouldn't do the shit Macon had. The woman who knelt before me was bare to me in all ways. I just had to prove her lack of guilt to my boss. That was the only way we could both be free.

North came up onto her knees. For a split second, I

thought she was going to stand, to walk away. But she only raised up so she could lick the drop of pre-cum from my dick.

My hand went to the back of her head and I tugged on her hair, forced her to meet my eyes as I lifted my hips, pushed my jeans down with my other hand.

My full length sprang free and was inches from North's face. Yet I kept my eyes on her. I saw everything there in those blue depths. Trust, desire, the need to please.

"My dirty princess." I slid my hand around, cupped her jaw, ran my thumb over her plump lower lip. Then I guided her to my dick and she took me in her mouth.

Fuck, I'd never seen anything hotter in my life. North, her hair mussed from my fingers, her eyes on mine as she hollowed her cheeks and took me into her mouth. I was too big for her to take all of me, but she sure as shit tried.

My hips bucked involuntarily, and I went too deep. Her eyes watered and she pulled back, breathing through her nose. I took her hand, wrapped her fingers around my base and let her at it again. She was voracious, drawing hot, wet pulls on me as if trying to suck the cum from my balls.

She'd do it too if she kept at it. And not for long.

I pulled her off me and she looked up at me with surprise, then confusion, then worry. As if I wasn't satisfied.

Taking her hand, which had been on my thigh, I stood, helping her to her feet. Then pointed. "Bed. Now."

"But—"

"Unless your pussy's sore from earlier, I'm taking it again." I went over to the side of her bed, pointed at the end table. "Got some toys in here?"

She nodded. I took that as permission to open the drawer. Besides a paperback, a packet of tissues and a tube of lip balm, I found her stash. Those battery-operated boyfriends that got her off.

I pointed at the bed again, waited for her to crawl her way up from the bottom.

I picked up the small vibrator, lipstick sized, dropped it on the bed right beside where she laid down. Her light hair fanned out across her pillow. Next I grabbed the larger vibrator, which had some kind of suction thing on the end.

I lifted the big dildo last, realistic with a thick vein running up the underside, but supersized as if molded from a porn star's dick. "You take this one for a ride?"

She nodded, her cheeks flushing so prettily. The

pink color spread down her neck and to the swells of her breasts.

I tossed it over my shoulder where it thudded on the carpet. "The only dick getting in that pussy from now on is mine."

Grabbing the second condom from my back pocket—thank fuck I'd been hopeful enough to bring two—I dropped it on the bed, then pushed off my pants.

Crawling over her, I set my hand by her head, leaned down and kissed her. Fuck she was sweet. I didn't linger on her lips, but kissed my way down her body, taking a minute to suck on her plump nipples, feeling them harden against my tongue. Then lower still, pushing her legs wide so I could settle between them.

"Jed," she breathed.

While it was just getting dark out, the room wasn't, her bedside lamp was on as well as the one by the window where I'd found her. I could see all of her, and this close, her pussy was wet, swollen from the hard fuck earlier, and all mine.

Reaching out, I grabbed the small lipstick vibrator. "This one first."

She looked down at me and frowned. "Um... what?"

"You're going to use this one first and I'm going to watch."

"No way."

I raised my hand, brought it down on her pussy in a light slap.

Her eyes flared wide and her back arched. A moan escaped her lips. I watched her closely, ensuring this was something she'd like. Yeah, it had been a test, but I had a feeling she'd get off on it, the slight bite of pain, the reprimand. It got her attention and got her out of her head. Her focus was all on me now, and her tingling pussy.

"Get busy, princess, or I'll spank your pussy again." Her eyes flared and a puff of air escaped her lips. "Not sure which you'd like better."

I raised my hand, but she grabbed the vibrator, twisted it so it began to buzz, and set it on her clit.

Her eyes fell closed and her knees flared wide.

My dick was leaking pre-cum all over her blanket. Just watching her use a vibe in just the way that got her off.

Fuck me.

I got my fingers involved, sliding one, then two into her as she kept at it.

"Don't come," I warned.

Her eyes flew open, and she looked at me with fury. I grinned. "You'll wait, princess."

I took her hand and set it back over her clit, then let go.

She might wait, but I couldn't. I shifted to my knees and slid the condom on as I watched her shift and writhe on her bed, lost.

I grabbed her hips, lined up at her entrance and thrust deep.

"Jed!" she cried.

I set her hand back on her clit, felt the vibrations in my dick as I began to fuck her. "Good girl. Come for me."

Her inner walls clamped down as she came, completely uninhibited. Wild.

I was going to come just watching her, and the feel of her milking my dick was enough to set me off, but I held back, let her come down from her pleasure.

I grabbed the little vibe from her hand, tossed it to the side. Grabbed the other vibrator next.

She stared at the thing wide eyed. "Oh no. I can't. Not with you in me too."

I thrust deep and her eyes fell closed.

"I'm not leaving you behind, princess." I set a ruthless pace, her bed slamming against the wall. "You've got one more in you. How are you going to come?"

She looked away.

I reached up, turned her face back so she met my eyes. I was buried deep, sweating, but I'd have all of her or none at all.

"What do you need? I'll give it to you."

She blinked.

"Just you and me."

Licking her lips, she reached out, grabbed the mini-vibe again. "Flip me over," she whispered.

I pulled out—fuck, that was hard to do—then helped her over onto all fours, then lowered her cheek to the bed so her ass was up. I could see all of her. *All.* Pink, swollen, wet. Grabbing her hips, I lined up, then slid into her in a slow, delicious stroke. I groaned at how deep I could go.

She moaned, then reached back to hand me the vibrator. "You."

I took it from her and took a second to understand

She clenched her butt, the muscles going taut, then relaxing. Her little rosebud also winked at me.

Ah.

She'd liked it when I'd touched her ass earlier. Fuck, the idea of taking that hole, claiming it as mine made my balls draw up. But she didn't want that. Yet. I hadn't told her that was an option. She was told to come with the vibrator and this was how.

It was still humming away so I ran it around where I was filling her, getting the tip of it coated in her juices. Then I sat it at her back entrance.

She startled, clenched. Cried out.

I set a hand beside her head, curved over her as I kept the little vibe just resting on that blatantly virgin hole. “Such a dirty princess. Does that feel good?” I murmured by her ear.

She nodded, then reached beneath herself and began fingering her clit.

“Such a good girl.”

I got busy then because I couldn’t hold back any longer. My woman was getting what she needed and by the way a sheen of sweat bloomed across her bare back, her inner walls squeezing and releasing, she was close to coming.

So was I. It was like a freight train, my orgasm, unable to stop for anything. I gritted my teeth and held off, pressing the vibe a little more intently against her sensitive flesh.

She cried out, deep and low as she came, her body tensing, then gushing satisfaction all over my dick. I thrust hard once, then twice, holding myself deep as I filled the condom. My fingers gripped her hips as I ensured that vibe and my dick hit every hot spot.

Only when she slumped into her blanket did I

twist the vibrator off and toss it aside, pulled out and tucked her into the bed. I took care of the condom in the bathroom and she didn't even move.

I smiled as I fixed the sheet and blankets around us, tucked her into my arms. She'd given herself to me. Fully. Completely. She might not even realize it yet. I'd seen the real North. Every inch of her and I wouldn't let her retreat now. No fucking way.

10

NORTH

I WOKE up like usual at five to crappy weather. And an empty bed. I reached out to touch the pillow where Jed had slept. Cold. I sat up, saw that his clothes weren't strewn on the floor.

He'd snuck out in the night. That meant several things. One, no one set the house alarm or Jed was a ninja and could sneak past it. Two, he'd left me sometime after he pretty much orgasmed me into unconsciousness.

I didn't think he'd gone out to get batteries for my vibrators we'd used. Or coffee, since the nearest town was ten miles away. He could be in the kitchen trying to figure out how to make some with Macon's fancy machine, but no. He wasn't here. I could... sense it.

He had a presence, some kind of magnetic pull that I couldn't resist.

I went to the window, naked, and looked out at the rain. The sky was starting to lighten, but there would be no sun. A gust of wind had water pummeling the window. The helicopter would be grounded so I'd be driving in today, which meant I had to skip my usual exercise.

Turning on the shower, I realized I didn't care. My muscles were a little achy, in some places more than others. I'd had my workout the night before. I stepped under the hot spray. Closed my eyes.

All I could see was Jed. His piercing stare, his drive to know all my secrets. To get me to reveal them to him. I hadn't uttered the truth of what Macon had done. Ever.

Until him.

South, East, and West were going to want to talk. To strangle me for keeping them in the dark all these years. Then they were going to want to know what Jed was to me, because not only had the guy been the one to get me to talk, they had to know he'd spent the night.

Or at least *part* of it.

I'd never once had a man at the house, not that my brothers were around to know that.

Why was I drawn to Jed? Why did I bare my soul to him? My body too.

I'd gotten on my knees for him. Let him order me around. Take control.

And I barely knew anything about him except what I'd learned from the workup on him. I knew about his family. That he went into the FBI. I pretty much had his bio until he was twenty-seven, when I'd seen him at his family's barbecue. The rest I got from the report. He'd worked at the FBI until a few months ago. Fired. Laid off. Something like that because of disciplinary action.

That didn't seem like the Jed I knew. But he worked for Marshall now. Shady characters flocked to shady characters.

But Jed wasn't shady. Was he? Nothing he'd said while we were together made me think that at all. Perhaps the opposite, too honorable. Was I falling for a guy like Macon? Was I replacing one asshole in my life for another? Was he giving me attention because he wanted something from me? I'd asked him that over and over and every single time he'd gotten pissed. Then chipped away a little more at my secrets. Even the dirty, kinky ones. While he kept his quiet.

Except he'd said he wanted me. All of me. That I was his. That my *pussy* was his. He touched me in so many different ways. Arms wrapped around me protectively. An ass spanking to get me to talk. A pussy spanking to remind me who was in control. Fingers skillfully finding my g-spot with the need to satisfy. His dick fucking me to make me submit, to dominate, to rule.

I'd signed the contract with Marshall. If that was Jed's sole motivation of coming to the wake, which he'd admitted, then he'd be done with me. I'd know all of it had been for a reason other than... than what? Love?

I finished my shower and went about getting ready for work. By the time I was dressed in another crisp dress and matching heels, I'd pushed away thoughts of why Jed wanted to be with me, because I was afraid of the truth. I'd survived Macon. I wasn't sure if I would survive Jed.

I found my brothers in the kitchen, clearly waiting for me. East and West were sitting on stools at the far end of the island drinking coffee. West had on a ratty t-shirt and East was bare chested. They looked hungover. Maybe they were.

South was dressed. Jeans and a white snap shirt. He held two travel mugs and handed one to me.

I stopped in my tracks, but Eddie went over to East and nudged him for a pet.

"What's this?" I asked.

"We need to talk," South said. His hair was damp as if he'd just gotten out of the shower. I didn't know if he'd come from his place or if he'd stayed in the guest house, which was more than big enough for him and East. I figured the latter.

"We want to talk to you, too," East began, then gave West a miserable glance. "But we feel like shit. South's going first. We'll hit you up later." He stood, West followed as they went into the great room and flopped down on the couches. West flung his arm over his eyes and groaned.

"I have to go to work," I told South. "With the bad weather, Paul grounded the helicopter." Paul was the pilot, who'd sent me an early morning text, as usual, if it was a no-go.

He shoved a to-go cup at me. "I'll drive."

Eddie was at my heels. He seemed to know the days I drove and always wanted to tag along. Everyone in the office loved him.

South headed for the garage, and I had no choice but to follow. He was mad at me. I didn't blame him, but nothing was going to change. I opened the back door of the car and Eddie jumped in. He did a circle, then sat down and stared at me, his tongue hanging out.

South didn't say much for the first few minutes of the ride, letting me sip my coffee in peace. The wipers were hypnotic, and the sound of the rain drowned out the radio.

"What's up with Jed Barnett?" he asked finally. "Do we need to beat the shit out of him?"

Slowly, I turned to face him, leaned against the door of the SUV. It was the car he'd chosen from the three I rotated driving, depending on mood and weather.

"Out of everything from last night, you want to know about Jed?"

"You didn't tell us much," he countered, giving me a death glare. Yeah, he wasn't happy. "Why the fuck did you save us?"

So much for talking about Jed.

"Because I had the power to do so."

He chewed on that for a bit. I watched as he strangled the steering wheel and ground his back molars. "There's so much to unpack in that sentence, I don't know where to start. So I won't. Right now," he added, making sure he knew we weren't done. "Jed Barnett."

"Yeah, Jed Barnett," I repeated.

"He seems to be able to handle you."

I returned his death glare. "*Handle* me?"

"You're too fucking strong."

"You make me out to be a bitch, which is totally sexist, by the way."

He gave me a look. "Don't put words in my mouth. You need a big guy to shoulder some of that load for you and spank your ass for what you did."

I looked out the side window because I could feel my cheeks heat. No way was I telling him that had already happened. "Have you heard yourself talk before? No wonder you're single."

"You're the fucking CEO of a billion-dollar company. You eat nails for breakfast. You put up with Macon, solo, for over a decade. I'm not sure if I'm ever going to forgive you for that."

He paused and I turned to look at him. Bad idea, because the steering wheel was going to have finger dents in it. He looked back at the road, put the blinker on to make a turn just outside of town for the road to the highway.

"We're not going over this again, are we?" I asked.

"Again? We never went over it. It's not like you ever ran it by any of us. You've always been so uptight."

I bristled at that and my spine went straight.

"So serious. Now I know why. You got three brothers out of that fucking house. All by yourself. Me wanting a man for you who's got big enough balls to understand all that and still wants to wrap his arms around you isn't being a chauvinistic asshole. It's our turn to protect you."

"Fine, but why Jed?"

"Because the short amount I've met the guy, he can hold his own with you. You need a guy who's stronger than you."

That definitely was Jed.

"Maybe he'll take you bowling or something."

I laughed at that. "Bowling?"

He looked me over. "Yeah, the shoes might be a problem for you."

I pursed my lips because I didn't have a response to that one. He was right. About the stupid bowling shoes and Jed. Jed had done nothing to stifle me. In fact, in a way, he'd liberated me. Set me free from—

The front window shattered. I jumped in surprise. South swore and tugged on the wheel, which had the SUV doing a one-eighty, tires squealing on the wet pavement. Even though I wore my seat belt, my head smacked the side window.

With the windshield being tempered, only a small amount of shards fell on us, but rain came through a hole in the center.

The SUV came to a shuddering stop, then South

gunned the engine, speeding off in the opposite direction. A *thump* hit the back of the vehicle.

"Get down!" South shouted, reaching out and shoving my head down between my legs.

"What's going on?" I cried, looking up at my brother. I thought he'd been pissed before, but I'd never seen him look like this.

"Someone's shooting at us," he snapped as the back window shattered.

11

JED

THE ONE THING I'd learned about North Wainright was that she could only be pushed so far. And I'd been doing some serious pushing. She'd fallen asleep in my arms, naked and sated. What we'd done... fuck, what she'd done, given over her control like she had, should have made me strut and preen like a prized bull in a field full of cows in heat.

It only made me lie awake beside her, stare up at the ceiling and listen to the weather roll in.

The things I'd pulled out of her made me want to kill her father with my bare hands. Too bad the fucker was already dead. He'd gotten off easy with a heart attack. Then there was the Texas oilman who'd been ready and willing to fuck his crony's daughter as part of a deal. I was going to find out who it was and finish him.

Everyone thought Billionaire Ranch was the place to live. Like royalty or some shit. The house was enormous. It had a fucking telephone room. The Wainrights lived in luxury. People to take care of every whim. I had to wonder if North even knew where the grocery store was or how to use a washing machine. She rode in a fucking helicopter to work.

But I'd bet my left nut she'd give it all up, every penny, for a normal and happy childhood. Her mother to have stayed alive. A father who protected and cherished his little girl instead of pimping her out. Money didn't buy happiness.

Even as I slipped from her bed and put on my clothes, I knew North was mine. After what she'd shared with me, how she'd gotten on her knees for me... there was no going back.

But like a skittish mare, I'd break her in slowly.

And while I was patient, I'd make Marshall happy and the FBI director satisfied that North had no involvement in her father's shady dealings. That the investigation into Wainright Holdings and North herself were finished.

That I was no longer undercover. That I was the man who held her while she slept. Who kept her safe from her past, and anything that happened for the rest of her life.

I drove home in the dark, showered and was about to call in to the office in DC, two hours ahead, when my cell rang. I saw the name and I smiled.

North was going to either rip a strip of hide off my ass for sneaking out or ask me to come back and fuck her some more.

My dick got hard for both, because I loved that sharp tongue of hers. She was learning how I took care of her sass. She liked it... eventually.

"Princess, I was just thinking—"

"Jed."

The hairs on the back of my neck stood up. I hopped out of my desk chair at the tone. Stared out the window as if I could see her through the rain. The view wasn't as spectacular as at Billionaire Ranch, but I had three hundred acres of prime grazing land with a creek running through it. Not too shabby.

"What's the matter?"

"Tell him we're coming to his house." It was one of her brothers on speaker, but I couldn't tell which one. Not yet.

"We're—"

"I heard," I said, cutting her off. "What the fuck is going on?"

I could hear the sound of an engine revving, the squeal of tires.

"Someone shot at us."

Shot?

"At the edge of town at the turn for the highway," her brother finished.

I knew the location. Everyone on the west side of the Wainright property took the same route to the interstate. There was a cluster of businesses there. A gas station, a small, local motel, and a restaurant.

"Anyone hurt?" I asked, going to my kitchen and retrieving my gun. While I knew it was loaded, I checked the cartridge anyway. Once satisfied, I went to the gun safe in my father's old den. Since there were no children in the house and my neighbors were a half a mile away, I kept the door closed, but unlocked.

"I've been hit but—"

"South? What the fuck!" North swore.

So she was with South. All three brothers had level heads, even after what they'd learned what North had done for them. Or what Macon had planned to do.

It had been clear they loved their sister, even though the relationship had been strained because of their father.

"I'm fine. It's a scratch," South said. "Eddie okay?"

"Your arm's bleeding!"

"Eddie?" South asked again. The dog was in the car with them.

"He's fine, you idiot. He's lying on the floor."

"Princess, you hurt?" I asked. I had to know.

"No. No, I'm fine."

My blood pressure dropped out of stroke level, but until I had her in my arms, I wasn't going to be calm.

"Jed, I have no idea who the fuck that was, or why," South said. His voice was rough, but he was calm. "It wasn't a fucking hunter's stray bullet. Not in July and not three shots."

South's words told me everything I needed to know. This was intentional and my woman was the target.

"I don't think we're being followed, but I'm not heading back to the ranch. Not sure if it's some kind of ambush or what the fuck. I need directions to your place. We're heading west on the county road."

I told him the way, which was fairly simple. There weren't that many roads out here.

"Princess, I'll be waiting."

Even though South had been the one talking, and shot, North was my top priority.

By the time I saw the fancy SUV fly down the dirt drive, I had shit pulled together and was ready.

South pulled up out front and I went to the passenger door and tugged it open. I was instantly wet from the rain, but I didn't give a shit. Reaching in, I unclipped North's seatbelt and pulled her from the car. She opened the back door and Eddie hopped out. With my gun in one hand and holding hers with the other, I pulled her inside, Eddie following. No way a shooter could know where South headed, follow and get into position to shoot again.

South slammed the front door shut behind him, leaned against it. His breathing was ragged. I scanned him and saw the blood oozing down his arm. If he said it was a scratch, I believed him.

My dog, Boozer, came in and checked everyone out. He and Eddie circled each other and wagged their tails. Instant friends.

I ignored them and looked at North, then ran my hands over her. She was in sky high stilts and another one of her dresses that probably cost more than my pickup truck. It was sexy as fuck and reminded me of how feminine she was. While she might be able to shoot like Annie Oakley, she needed to be treated like a precious piece of glass. Deserved it.

"You okay?" I asked when I was finally satisfied she

had no bullet holes. I cupped her cheeks, leaned down and met her gaze.

Her pupils were blown, but she was calm. Her hair was damp, her skin dotted with rain drops. Her nipples poked against the dark silk.

She winced when my fingers pressed into her scalp.

"I whacked my head on the window," she admitted.

I felt a little goose egg with my fingertips.

"Got a first aid kit?" South asked.

"Kitchen table," I replied, not looking away.

I heard South cut across the living room, the dogs following.

"Time to go, princess."

She frowned. "Go?"

I nodded. "Gotta get you somewhere safe until we know what the fuck is going on."

I had a cabin up in the hills no one knew about. She'd be safe there.

She shook her head, stepped back. I let her go. She turned and went into the kitchen. I followed.

South was shrugging out of his shirt. I saw the thin slice a bullet made across his deltoid. It must hurt like a bitch and would ooze blood unless bandaged. He'd probably need a few stitches and a course of antibiotics, but he'd be fine, and have a nice scar to remember the event.

"Oh my God," North said, digging her shaky hands into the kit to look for something. I had a feeling she didn't even know what.

I grabbed a kitchen towel that was draped over the oven door handle, gave it to South. He pressed it to his wound.

"You need to get her out of here. Away," South said, his eyes meeting mine. They were deadly serious. Angry.

I nodded. "Already on it. I've got a place."

North gave up on her search and spun on her high heel. Her wide eyes met mine, then South's. "Away?"

"They sure as shit weren't shooting at me," South said, holding the towel to his arm. "Jed's going to protect you while we figure out what's going on."

"We?" North asked, clearly confused.

"Your brothers," South countered. "The three guys you saved. It's time to save you right back."

"But—"

"You're going with Jed," South commanded.

I'd kidnap North from her own brother if he'd said anything else. Thank fuck I didn't have to cold cock a guy who'd been shot and do so.

"We should call the police," North replied. While

she appeared calm, I couldn't miss the way her hands shook. She was probably used to working well under pressure, but there was a big difference between a cutthroat business deal and being shot at.

This was where I excelled. It was my job to save people from the bad guys. I'd been trained to do so. I'd left in the middle of the night to give her space and time. That was fucking gone now. The schedule had been moved up. The second I saw her at that wake, I knew I was fucked. That I didn't give a shit if she were guilty or not. She was my woman.

I'd remained undercover, kept that a secret even after what we'd done. Until now.

North Wainright was more important than my job. More important than anything else in the world.

So I told her the truth. Even if she hated me, I was the best one to keep her alive. Then I could grovel and do whatever it took. People said make up sex was the best. I hoped I'd find out.

"I am the police," I said.

South stilled, narrowed his eyes.

North shook her head. "Yeah, I know you got fired from the FBI, but that doesn't do us any good. We need law enforcement now."

I went over to North, took the tube of antibiotic

ointment I hadn't even realized she'd been holding, dropped it on the kitchen table.

"South, there's a burner phone on the table for you. I programmed in my number. You can reach us on it."

"Got it," he replied.

Her blue eyes were wild, but she was calm. Relatively. Her car had been shot up and her brother had a bullet graze on his arm. I was calm too. Relatively.

"South's going to call your brothers to pick him up while we get the fuck out of here." I glanced at him, who nodded.

"We need the police!" she repeated.

"Princess, I didn't get fired from the FBI. I'm back in Montana undercover. None of that matters."

She stared at me wide eyed. "Undercover? None of that matters?" she practically screeched.

"You're my woman, that's what matters. I sure as shit am going to protect you."

I wouldn't shame her kink in front of her brother by reminding her who was in charge. Me being in control might get her off, but it also kept her safe.

"Say goodbye to your brother, grab a rifle, get your perfect ass out to my garage and climb in my truck."

"You can't be serious."

"If I have to toss you over my shoulder, I will."

South laughed.

North whipped her head around to get help from her brother. "You can't expect me to go off with him!"

"If he doesn't carry you to his truck, I will. I love you, North. Go with your man."

North sputtered, turned a pretty shade of pink, then did what she was told. Thankfully, she didn't shoot *me* with the gun before we sped off into the hills, Eddie and Boozer in the back seat.

12

NORTH

I DIDN'T SAY a word as Jed drove us deep into the mountains. We skirted Wainright land most of the way, but then turned south. I'd never been in this area before and since we hadn't passed another car in ten minutes, it seemed not many did. But Jed knew where he was going, taking lefts and rights so I wasn't sure if I could drive my way back out.

The rain had let up and only drips from over-hanging pines splashed on the windshield. Jed slowed the truck and turned down a single lane road, the entry narrow and between two lodgepole pines. We meandered through the forest, a tire catching a deep rut here and there, before we drove into a clearing. There, settled in a field of Montana wildflowers was a small cabin. The walls were log. On the front side, two windows flanked the front door. I pegged it as one room with a porch that went around three sides. It was rustic, but well kept. It was the view though, that made this place.

Where the main house of the Wainright Ranch had been built for sweeping views in all directions, the cabin felt secluded. The field was perhaps two acres and when I was out of the truck, I heard water running. A creek cut across the side and into the woods. With the clouds breaking and the sun coming out, it was beautiful. Quiet. Serene.

"What is this place?" I asked.

Jed opened the back door of his quad cab for the dogs and they hopped out, ran off to explore.

"My cabin."

I looked away from the view and to Jed. He pulled a bag and tossed it over his shoulder.

"This place is yours?"

He nodded, walked across the flagstones to the front door. It had a keypad lock and he pushed a few of the numbers to unlock it. He pushed it open and turned to face me. Waited.

He was rugged as always. Jeans and sturdy work

boots. Today he wore a black t-shirt and his Stetson was missing. He looked like a lumberjack, only needing to replace the duffel bag he carried with an axe. The setting was perfect. He fit here.

I cut past him inside and he followed, set the bag down.

As I took in the interior, he walked around, opening windows and the sliding door at the back. As I'd thought, it was one large room, although there was a small bathroom with a door to my right. The kitchen had a fridge and stove/oven combo, a sink that overlooked the field. A small butcher block island. There was no dishwasher, only a drying rack. There was a large fireplace surrounded by river rock. A leather couch faced it and an overstuffed chair and ottoman were in the corner. I could see Jed here in the dead of winter, fire blazing, dog at his feet, as he read. In the far corner was a large bed, the frame hewn also from logs. A quilt covered it and one hung on the wall above the headboard.

A thick rug covered the floor in front of the fireplace and couch, but the rest was bare wide-plank beams. The space had been stuffy being closed up, but there was a breeze coming through the windows which set the simple muslin curtains fluttering.

Someone had built this place by hand and I guessed it was Jed.

"Did you build this?"

He shrugged, glanced around. "My father and I. I bought the land after college. When I came home to visit, we'd work on it. Some things we hired out, like the foundation and the chimney. My mother had her hand in decorating."

I couldn't imagine Jed choosing navy throw pillows for the leather sofa or cafe curtains. Her touch had been gentle though because her touches didn't make it feminine, only charming.

"It's really great, Jed."

His eyes widened as he turned them to me. "It's not Billionaire—"

I held up my hand. "Don't even finish that. You think I'm too... snooty for this?" Then I waved my hand around to take in his place.

His gaze raked over me. "If the shoe fits, princess."

I looked down at myself, took in my business dress, my heels. I looked ridiculous dressed as I was, where I was. Lifting my foot, I grabbed one heel, tugged it off, dropped it to the floor. Then did the other.

"I didn't have time to pack a bag. It's this or naked."

His eyes flared with heat as he looked me over once more, definitely imagining me naked.

"While that's going to happen, you being naked, we've got to talk first."

"*We*? I'm not the liar."

"You sure about that?"

"What does that even mean? You fucked me... to what? Get answers?"

"I fucked you to get you off. Because I couldn't wait another second to get my dick in you."

The words were hot, but empty. "You *used* me."

He ran a hand over his beard, sighed. "If I remember correctly, you were the one bent over your daddy's desk with my mouth on your pussy."

"I... I—" I had no idea what to say. Suddenly I was so angry I was sure smoke was coming out of my ears. "You might be pissed about what Macon did, but he only fucked me over. He didn't *actually* fuck me."

If molars could be ground to dust, his probably would. I had a feeling he wanted to say something back. Instead, he went to the duffel, opened the zipper and rummaged around. "Here, princess. This is the best I can do." He handed me a t-shirt and thick socks. Tipped his head toward the bathroom. "Get changed and we'll talk."

He left me standing there, heading out onto the porch, the screen door slapping shut behind him. The dogs ran up the steps and circled around him to get pets. Jed's dog—one I didn't even know he had—held a stick in his mouth. Jed grabbed it and flung it out into the field. Both dogs ran after it.

Did I look so adoringly at Jed, where he tossed something out, like affection or orgasms and I ran after them, again and again?

I groaned, then stomped off to the bathroom to change. He was right. We had talking to do. The bathroom was small with a sink, clawfoot tub and toilet. A matching braided rug was on the floor. Navy towels were folded neatly on a shelf above the toilet and a matching hand towel on a hook beside the sink.

I didn't know how often Jed came to the cabin, but it was tidy and clean. Definitely not a bachelor pad like East's place in Bozeman. I hadn't even seen a TV.

I stripped off my damp dress and put on his t-shirt. It was gray and had FBI in huge black letters across my chest. It was also soft and smelled like laundry and Jed and was huge on me, reminding me how big the guy was. I laid my dress out over the shower curtain rod. It was too warm for the socks, so I kept them rolled up and dropped them back in the open duffel on the way by.

Jed was in an Adirondack chair, a foot propped up

on the railing when I came out. He looked me over, but didn't say anything. The dogs were at his feet, sprawled out. Eddie saw me but didn't move more than a tail wag.

"What's your dog's name?"

"Boozer."

The dog lifted his head at being called, licked his chops, then flopped back down. I'd guess he was a mutt, but had some kind of hunter in him. His fur was brown with patches of lighter fur.

"I got you some water." He pointed to two glasses that were set on a chunk of log used as a little side table. There was also a dishtowel there, and since the other chair was dry, I assumed he used it to wipe them down after the rain. I dropped into the comfortable seat and took a big gulp of the water. It was cool and fresh, either from a well or a spring.

"Do we even have food out here?" I asked.

"We might be in the middle of nowhere, but there's electricity. Propane. The freezer's full of ready-made meals. We won't starve. I know you've got a lot of questions, princess."

He wasn't asking so I stayed quiet.

"I'll start at the beginning. I was recruited for the FBI in college, which you know."

I nodded, setting the glass down.

"What you also know is that I was fired for taking bribes from corrupt officials and well... the bad guys." He stood, turned and leaned against the railing so he faced me. "I wasn't fired. I was assigned a new case. Macon Wainright."

My head whipped up in surprise. "What?"

"He's been under investigation for the past year, but it wasn't getting anywhere. They needed someone on the inside. Someone undercover."

"You."

He nodded. "It's not like any agent could do that out here. He—or she—would have to blend in. Have a believable story."

Jed had been born and raised in the area. A cowboy before he'd become an agent.

"What's the saying?" I said. "You can't take the cowboy out of the agent but you can take the agent out of the cowboy?"

The corner of his mouth tipped up. "Something like that."

"It's just coincidence you grew up where your investigation was," I said, thinking about how small of a world it was.

His jaw clenched, then released. "One hell of a coincidence, which my boss was thrilled about. I was the only one for the job. My cover was easy to make because almost all of it was true. People remember me."

I flushed, because I'd remembered him from all those years ago. I'd believed his cover.

"So as part your cover you came back and got a job with John Marshall to gain access to Macon through him."

A bird flew over, cried out, then swooped into the woods.

"Yes."

My mind worked through all the possibilities of what Macon could have done to bring him into the FBIs radar. "What is it you think he did?"

They wouldn't have been investigating my father for a year if they didn't consider him a suspect of a crime. And to send Jed undercover—

"The FBI is federal. We only handle certain kinds of cases. Terrorism."

My mouth fell open. "Terrorism? You think—"

He held up a hand. "No. We also specialize in white collar crimes and public corruption. Macon was good at being bad, North. The CEO of a billion-dollar company was talented at keeping his hands clean."

I knew that. I figured he'd stop at nothing to close a deal, even using me, but I'd never known him to do things illegal. Unethical, definitely.

"He's dead. Your case is closed. Why are you still here?"

I swallowed, not sure if I wanted the answer. Was he leaving? Did I want him to? I hated him, or so I thought. I didn't know what real was any longer.

"Because the case shifted. To the new CEO."

13

NORTH

I HOPPED to my feet and he grabbed me before I could storm off. His arm banded my waist and he pulled me back against him. I wished I still had on my heels so I could jam one into the top of his foot.

"Let me go!" I struggled, but he wasn't going to let me go.

"You didn't do it," he said, his voice a snarl in my ear.

"I don't even know what *it* is."

"You didn't do it," he repeated.

I stared at the logs that built the house, the screen door. "I heard you the first time. You'd have arrested me if you had evidence that I did... whatever. Which means, I want to know what information you're fucking me for."

He let go of me as if I'd burned him.

I stalked across the deck, crossed my arms over my chest.

"Marshall bought a piece of land by the Canadian border," Jed began. "He bought it for Macon because the owner wouldn't sell it to your father. We don't know the reason. Maybe because he was a shifty asshole. We do have record of the sale to Marshall. We also have a contract Macon signed with the intent to purchase the land from him."

I stilled because what he was saying was fact. I knew all this because I'd finalized that deal the night before. Got Julian to ensure the funding was wired to Marshall. I'd done it not to make Marshall happy, but to see where Jed stood. If he'd walk away once the job for his boss was done.

Turned out, that wasn't even his actual job.

"You know what I'm talking about," he said, studying me.

I nodded, licked my lips. "Yes. That's not illegal."

"No, it's not. It's what Macon planned to do with the land that we're interested in."

"Any land Wainright Holdings purchases is for

conservation. It would have been donated to a land conservancy group."

Jed leaned back against the rail once more, slowly shook his head. "Our intel says he's planning to lease the land to a logger. Then to a company that strip mines."

"No. No, that's not true. He can't do that. There are laws."

"The FBI investigates white collar crimes and public corruption," he repeated.

I bit my lip. Considered.

"You knew Macon better than anyone. Don't you think this is something he'd do?"

It sounded just like him. "I'm the head of the company's philanthropy. I know nothing about this."

"What he was planning wasn't very philanthropic," he countered.

The calmer he got, the more riled I became. This had Macon written all over it. He'd kept me in the dark, because I would have fought him on it. "Fine. He's dead. None of it matters now."

"Except if he made the deals with government officials and those loggers on the condition the land was purchased."

Oh shit.

Had I just set in motion the destruction of hundreds of acres of pristine wilderness?

"I knew nothing about that," I said, refusing to tell him that I'd closed the contract with Marshall. The purchase wasn't illegal, especially if I did actually donate it to a conservation group.

I hadn't seen the contract with the loggers or whatever the company was. It hadn't been in the pile Julian had given me the day before. I could only imagine where it was and if Macon had a secret stack of deals he never wanted me to know about.

Of course he did. I'd have to find it and ensure this one was never signed because the land was to be preserved, not destroyed.

"I know," he said.

"Say it is real. This... deal. It's as dead as Macon without my signature."

"Maybe. That's why my boss has kept me in."

"In me, you mean." I closed my eyes, shook my head. "This started when you came to the wake. You admitted you were there for Marshall. The goal then was to fuck me to... what, sign the land contract, right?"

I saw him wince.

I took a deep breath, let it out, tried not to cry. God, this man pulled every emotion from me. I felt things.

So many things with him and not all of them were good. He could somehow heal me of old wounds one minute and destroy me with new ones the next.

"But that wasn't all. You came back for more for your other boss. The FBI." I sniffed. "Wow, the bed was more crowded than I thought last night."

He groaned, rubbed his beard. "Marshall sent me to the wake and told me to fuck you for answers. Since Macon was dead, he was out millions on that land purchase and needed to know if you'd still buy it."

I didn't expect him to actually admit it.

He took a step toward me, and I stepped back.

"The moment I saw you coming down those stairs at the wake, everything changed."

"So you didn't want to fuck me. Could've fooled me."

Tears lodged in my throat and I swallowed hard.

"That was what I was told to do. Not what I was *going* to do. We're a little alike, aren't we?"

I pursed my lips. "I have no idea how." I took in his rugged physique and I felt so small in comparison.

"We had orders to fuck to get others what they wanted."

"The difference is that Texas oil tycoon wouldn't have taken no for an answer."

I thought I heard him growl. "I want that asshole's name."

Laughing, I said, "So you can beat him up?"

"Put him in jail."

He was dead serious and that... made me feel good. But I hated him.

"Fine. You changed your mind about doing what Marshall commanded. What about your real boss at the FBI? I'm sure he—"

"She," he corrected.

"She's not too thrilled about you sleeping with a suspect."

"She doesn't know. I don't kiss and tell."

I studied him. Eddie stood up, went over to a bowl of water in the corner of the porch and drank sloppily.

"You are a terrible employee," I said finally.

He smiled, but it didn't reach his eyes. "No kidding. Marshall still owns a piece of land he doesn't want and the FBI can't connect you to any crimes."

Jed didn't know about the signed contract, which meant he hadn't talked to Marshall this morning.

"You dragged me out here to what, force me to sign the contract my father made with Marshall and then have me open all my files so you can dig through them? It's either that or jail?"

"You're here because someone shot at you. Tried to kill you."

"I'm not good to you dead," I countered.

He stared at me, wide-eyed, then ran a hand down over his face, through his beard. It was his obvious sign of frustration.

"Jesus, woman. You have no idea how special you are. How amazing. So fucking strong. Stubborn. Frustrating."

"Yay, what every woman wants to he—"

He closed the distance between us and settled his palm over my mouth, hooked his other hand around my back.

"You're here because I'm protecting you. Because it's my job to do so. Not working for Marshall or the FBI. Because I'm your man."

He pulled his hand away and kissed me. Like I was water and he'd trekked through the desert. Like he was my man. Like... I was his and he was proving it.

Eventually, he broke the kiss, set his forehead against mine.

"I saw you at the wake and decided then and there you were mine. I never forgot you from that barbecue when you were there with Jock. I was attracted to you then. Never went away."

Oh.

"Do you think I wanted to fall in love with the woman who Marshall expected me to fuck and that my boss has me undercover investigating?"

"What?" I stared at him, appalled.

"When you first mentioned that you'd gotten info on me, I told you not to believe everything you read. I wanted to tell you the truth. I couldn't." His dark gaze dropped to my lips. "I love you, North Wainright. That's no lie."

"You can't," I whispered. Those three words were the last thing I'd expected him to say. *Anyone* to say.

"I can. I'll spend the rest of my life proving it."

"This is insane," I sputtered. I was more shocked now than when I'd been told Macon had died.

He growled. "Insane is still arguing with you." The next thing I knew, I was tossed over his shoulder. He went inside, the screen door slapping shut behind him. He grabbed something from a kitchen drawer, then cut across the room to the bed. Dropped me on it.

I bounced and popped back up.

"Jed. What do you mean the rest of your life?"

"You've got an MBA, I think you understand."

"We barely know each other and I don't even know who you really are."

He stood at the foot of the bed, crossed his arms over his chest. "You know exactly who I am."

"You lied to me!"

"You lied to your brothers."

My mouth fell open, then shut. "These are nothing alike. You can't say you haven't been trying to find evidence of my guilt."

"I told you. You didn't do it. You're not involved in Macon's shit. I know it."

"You have proof?" I couldn't miss the hope in my words.

"No, but I have you. I believe in you. Ever since the wake, I've been trying to find evidence of your innocence."

"So besides someone shooting at me, I have to worry the FBI is going to put me in jail for taking over for Macon?"

His jaw clenched. "We don't know it's not your brothers trying to kill you."

I heard what he said. Processed it, yet my brain stalled. "My brothers?" I whispered.

"How often does South drive you to work?" he asked.

"Never."

"The one time he takes you, you're shot at."

"He got shot!"

"That's what happens when bullets start flying," he countered.

"Why... I don't understand. They... why—"

"Why would your brothers want you dead? I can think of a billion reasons."

I shook my head, my heart numb. I hadn't been all that close with them, but there was a big difference between not sending birthday presents and murder.

"They don't need my money. They have trusts of their own from our mother. Her family built the house. Built the empire. Macon was just the ranch hand."

"You have more shares in the company."

I laughed, imagining my brothers in suits working at the office. "They don't want anything to do with the company. It's not them. Not for money. They have plenty."

"You have more." He eyed me because he hadn't asked. He assumed it was fact.

I nodded. "I have more shares. I make a big salary. Get bonuses. But their trusts aren't skimpy." Jed knew I was rich. Knew the nickname Billionaire Ranch was accurate, yet we'd never used actual numbers. "They each have hundreds of millions of dollars, and that's without any kind of investing or growth."

Jed whistled.

"It's not them," I said. "You want me to trust people. I am. I trust my brothers."

He eyed me, then nodded.

"Fine. We'll connect with them later, see what they found out about the shooter. If you can access your files remotely, we can dig around. See what we can find on Macon's deal with the loggers. But now..."

He raised his hand, let a pair of handcuffs dangle.

My mouth fell open as I stared at the shiny metal.

"You're arresting me?"

Shaking his head, his gaze raked down my body. "All we can do now, princess, is wait. And I know just how to fill that time."

I stared at the cuffs, swallowed. "What?"

"No one's ever been able to get you off. There's nothing you have to do. No work. No phone calls. No yoga or swimming or shopping or manicure. No ranch hands to ask a question. No assistant."

"We just... what, have sex while we wait?"

"I'm not playing Scrabble with you."

"Jed," I said on a sigh, although my nipples were hard with anticipation.

"Do you have a better idea? Because I sure as fuck can't think of anything better than getting my mouth on that pussy."

Heat spread through my body. "Okay, so why the handcuffs?"

He dropped them on the bed, put one knee on the

mattress and lifted the t-shirt up and off me. His eyes slid over my pale-yellow bra and panty set, but he said nothing. Only reached behind me and deftly removed the bra.

"Because when you're cuffed to my headboard, you'll have no doubt who's in control."

He grabbed the cuffs, watched my eyes as he carefully snicked one closed about my wrist. I didn't say anything, but I also didn't tell him no. I'd never been into bondage. No one had ever tied me up during sex. Not even using a tie or a pair of nylons. The handcuffs and Jed... together? He was taking me places I'd never even considered, but definitely got me hot.

"Someone shot at me, Jed," I said, all of a sudden feeling very vulnerable.

Instead of hugging me or throwing something against the wall, he only nodded, ground his teeth together, and closed the handcuff around my other wrist.

He helped me lay back, raised my arms overhead. I wasn't sure how it worked, but the cuffs should have gone around the headboard.

Jed slid the belt from his jeans, then used that to wrap around the wood and then the chain of the handcuffs so my hands weren't near the thick logs. I tugged, testing. I wasn't going anywhere. I wasn't sure if I should be panicked or excited. I was… both.

"Fuck, look at you."

His gaze was heated, but filled with something like reverence, as if what he was looking at—*me*—was too beautiful to be real. All my concerns slipped away.

His eyes snapped to mine as he ran his hands up my calves. "Time for you to give me everything, princess. Your pleasure, too."

14

JED

I WAS USED to compartmentalizing shit. Cases and real life could be kept separate. Now they bled together. North was my case and my life. She'd been shot at. Someone wanted her dead. While she'd convinced herself it wasn't one of her brothers, I hadn't ruled that out. Yet. I'd have to update my boss, get North in her network. Check in with her brothers and see what they said. All of that.

But not now. Now I had North away from everything. I had a feeling this moment was like a unicorn. I couldn't miss out on the opportunity to have my woman completely and totally to myself. She was tied to my fucking bed with only one thing she had to focus on. An orgasm.

I had to wonder if she'd ever had an opportunity to stop thinking completely. It was obvious she'd never given herself to anyone fully. Not even me. Yet.

I'd push her, get her past places where she'd given up and used her fingers before. Where she didn't keep trusting or giving herself to someone to take care of her.

I'd try now. I'd watch her, but if she truly couldn't come, I wasn't going to make it worse. Watching North touch herself during sex was fucking hot. I was man enough to be okay with that the rest of my life as long as she screamed my name.

As she tested the handcuffs, I gripped her ankle, stroked her calf. "You good?"

Her eyes met mine. Wary, sure. Aroused, definitely. She licked her lips, then nodded.

I didn't think so much of myself that I was better than any guy she'd been with, that the reason any of them hadn't been able to get her off was because they sucked in the sack.

She hadn't been able to do it with me, either. I wasn't a sex therapist, but if she could come from just letting go… completely, then this was the time to test that theory.

We were off the grid. While we didn't have all the time in the world, we had enough.

My hands slid up the insides of her thighs, pushed her legs wide. With slow movements, I slid her pretty yellow panties down her thighs, tossed them over my shoulder. Before she could bring her knees back together, I settled my shoulders in the way, parted her with my thumbs.

"Prettiest fucking pussy."

"Jed," she whispered, squirming a little.

I gave her a light spank right over her clit. "No rushing me."

She lifted her head off the pillow, stared… no, *glared* down her naked body at me all the while her nipples pebbled and her pussy dripped her sweetness.

"Here's how this is going to work. You're going to feel. Scream, cry out, gasp. Moan. Wiggle. Whatever you want. But other than telling me to stop… no, not even that. You say red, princess, because you've got a problem. A legit one like the cuffs are hurting you."

"You want me to have a safe word?" she asked, her eyes wide.

"I want you to know you're safe," I countered,

continuing to slide my hands over her silky skin. "You're not in charge here. You don't have control. You don't have to do anything. I don't have to be anywhere but between your thighs. I'm in no rush. Got it?"

"You'll get bored if it takes too long."

I laughed at that. "Bored?" I pointed at her pussy. "Here? I could spend the rest of my life right fucking here."

She gave me a glare that I assumed she'd used in the past to make lesser men cower. "Yes. But I can't come without using my fingers on my clit."

Those words were a challenge. I wanted to tell her to *hold my beer* but, I didn't respond. Instead, I got to work. I hadn't been lying when I told her it was no hardship to eat her out. Her pussy was the sweetest thing in the world. Hot, wet. Plush. So pink. I had no idea how long I licked and fingered her, but she writhed and moaned, tugged on the cuffs and called out my name.

Sweat dotted her skin.

I took the time to learn how her clit liked to be flicked, the right press on her g-spot. Deep fingering versus shallow. Circling her entrance. Teasing. It was when I added a swirl of my thumb to her ass did things ramp up.

She was close, to the point where she could probably get herself over the finish line. The cuffs rattled and I knew she wanted to reach down and do just that.

I looked up her gorgeous body and she lifted her head. Looked at me. Then burst into tears.

I kissed my way up her body as she cried. I'd wanted a release from her, and I'd gotten one.

"Shh," I murmured, kissing one nipple and then the other, working my way to her cheeks.

"Jed!" she wailed.

"Pretty intense, huh?" I whispered, nibbling along her neck. "I've got you. You're safe."

The crying jag bled away pretty fast, and I set my hand beside her head, stared down at her.

She blinked her watery eyes open.

"Okay?" I asked.

She sniffed. "Yes."

"Good girl. I got to a good spot, but your release turned the wrong way. Ready for more?"

She stared at me with teary, confused eyes. "That's... you're not—"

"Far from done. Remember, nothing to do but get you off."

She nodded, took a deep breath.

I gave her a smile, kissed her, then pushed off the bed.

I stood, grabbed a condom from my pocket, stripped, then protected us both.

I moved back between her thighs and put my mouth on her again. She tasted so fucking good. "Jed, I thought—"

"Not in charge," I reminded, and made her lose her mind.

Only when she was worked back up again did I shift, thrust into her. Fucked her.

Then pulled out, ate her out, used my fingers. Then shifted back to giving her more of my dick.

I alternated, making her out of her mind. My balls were drawn up, watching her like this, lost to only what I made her feel, was intense. She was panting, moaning, wailing. Crying my name.

I flipped her onto her stomach, the belt connecting the cuffs to the headboard twisting and allowing the motion and pulled her up onto her hands and knees.

I settled behind, nudged her knees wide and slid back inside. "Now, princess. Come now."

I circled my thumb around where I filled her to coat it, then pressed it into her ass. At the same time, I reached around with the other hand, found her slippery clit and pinched it.

Her inner walls clamped down on me as she came. And came. Her fingers clawed at the bedding. Her toes curled. Her long hair clung to her sweaty back. Her inner walls milked my thumb and dick. She screamed, then went silent as her muscles went taut.

"Fuck yes," I breathed, pounding into her now, taking. Giving. Finding completion together.

15

NORTH

I FELL ASLEEP. Jed had removed the handcuffs and curled his big body around mine. Whispering how beautiful I was, how perfect, in my ear. Then I was out. I had no idea how long I slept, but not for too long. The sun was shining and I could hear Jed talking out on the porch.

I grabbed the FBI t-shirt from the floor and put it on, this time skipping the panties and bra and joined Jed outside.

His gaze raked over me as I stepped onto the deck. I didn't miss that he was only in his jeans. I hadn't been able to touch that rugged, muscled body earlier. My fingers itched to do so now.

The dogs were out in the field, sniffing around. They saw me, wagged their tails, then got back to whatever scent they were following.

"I agree," he said into the phone, curling his finger and beckoning me over. "Yes." He paused. "No idea."

I stopped in front of him and he banded an arm about my waist and set me on his lap. The angle of the Adirondack chair had me leaning back against him, my head resting on his chest. The arm wrapped around me cupped my bare thigh.

"It's South," he said, handing me the phone.

"Hi," I said once I put the cell to my ear.

"You doing okay?"

I left out the fact that Jed had handcuffed me to his bed and fucked an orgasm out of me. A man-induced one. South was pro-Jed, but that might change if he knew how he defiled me. Got me on my knees. It seemed I had a thing for ass play and it probably wouldn't be long before he worked more than his thumb in me there.

Then there was the fact that Jed thought South may be the one who wanted me dead.

"Yes," I replied. "Did you learn anything new?"

"I talked to the sheriff. We found spent casings on

the roof of the gift shop. Even though it's only one floor, it's got a ladder on the back."

I sighed, knowing that wasn't much, other than proving it had been intentional.

"Let us know if you learn anything else."

"I don't want you dead, North."

I turned and looked up at Jed. He could probably hear what South had said and didn't look the least bit sorry.

"I know," I replied, imagining the conversation they'd had while I'd been asleep.

"I want to beat the shit out of Jed for even thinking the three of us would hurt you, but he's protecting you. I respect that."

I sighed, realized South was right. In a backwards way, Jed was showing how much he cared. It didn't matter to him that the guys would hate him. That wasn't important to him.

I was.

"West and East say hi. Glad you're safe."

"Hi back."

South hung up and I handed the phone back to Jed. He set it on the little table, then tipped my chin up so I met his dark eyes. "You good, princess?"

I nodded, realizing I was, then cupped his jaw. Felt the soft rasp of his beard.

"I pushed you pretty hard."

I looked away and I felt my cheeks heat. "Yeah. But… God, it had been amazing."

He leaned down, kissed my nose. "We just need to get you out of that head of yours. We'll work on it, but know that it's sexy as hell watching you touch yourself."

"You like it as long as I come."

He kissed my forehead. "Every time. And often."

"Yeah, well. A lot is going on right now so we'll see what happens. We can't stay in this cabin forever."

His cell rang and he tipped it so he could read the display. Grunted. "My boss."

I assumed he meant the FBI boss and not John Marshall. And that meant our little bubble of isolation had burst.

"Director," he said. Not Marshall. "Yes. She's here with me. Yes. No. Yes, she knows. I'll put her on speaker."

Those few words lasted about a minute. Jed's face gave nothing away as his boss spoke. I sucked in a breath when he hit the button and held it between us.

"Go ahead," Jed said.

"Hello, North. This is Director Amy Sprouse. It seems you are aware of our investigation into your father."

"Into me, from what I understand," I replied, glancing at Jed, worried he'd be mad for pushing back on his boss. He offered me a small nod.

"Agent Barnett has shared quite a bit with you."

"I have," he said. "There are no secrets between us."

My heart skipped a beat at those words. He wasn't just telling them to me, but to a higher up at the flipping FBI.

"Are you sure?" she countered. "Did she tell you she signed the contract with John Marshall? That Wainright Holdings now owns the parcel of land that has been the recent focus of our investigation?"

Jed's fingers clenched my thigh and his eyes pierced into me.

"Last night," I said. "After."

I didn't explain more, but he knew based on the way I could feel my cheeks heat.

After the telephone room.

"I... needed to know if you were around for me or the land," I whispered.

His jaw clenched and he leaned in, murmured in my ear. "I should spank your ass for that. Do you doubt me now?"

My nipples went hard at the idea of him spanking me again. I shook my head.

"It will go to the nature group as part of our conservancy program," I told her.

"I believe her," Jed said.

I smiled. I couldn't help it. Someone wanted me dead and yet I couldn't be happier. Jed was on my side, and he'd given me the best orgasm of my life and—

"Then you're thinking with the wrong brain, Agent."

Jed blinked, looked to his phone. "What are you talking about?"

"North Wainright signed a contract leasing that land to Caston Logging," the director said.

I sucked in a breath. "No, I didn't."

Jed's gaze dropped to mine.

"Your signature is on it."

"How did you get a hold of it?" Jed asked his boss.

"We got a subpoena for the logging company's records. We've been poring over files ever since. Wasn't all that hard to find."

I felt Jed stiffen. "Why didn't you call me?"

"We did. You didn't answer."

I didn't know what time that was, but he'd been with me last night from dinner until before dawn.

"You also didn't check in this morning," she added.

"That's because someone tried to kill North. Shots fired at an intersection on the way to Billings."

There was a pause and we could hear her talking to someone else, as if she'd covered up the phone with a hand. "I'm glad to hear you are all right, Miss Wainright."

"Why? So I go to jail?"

"We have the evidence needed for Jed to arrest you."

He squeezed my thigh again, getting me to meet his gaze. He shook his head.

"I believe you," I whispered to him, meaning I knew he hadn't planned all of this. I would already be in his custody and already know what the feel of handcuffs was like.

"When did I sign this contract?" I asked. "From what Jed told me, the lease with a logging company would only become an option if the land was purchased. Since I signed the contract last night, I had to have done it since then."

"That's correct," she confirmed.

"If the contract was signed online, then it's a generic digital signature. And there's a time stamp," I said, very familiar with the arrangement. I was sure she was too.

"Nine thirty-four," she replied, as if reading it off of her computer.

My heart stuttered, literally skipped a beat and

adrenaline pumped through me. Sheer relief. Jed knew I hadn't signed that contract because I'd been handcuffed to his bed. But then realization struck. A scary one.

"I couldn't have signed it." I didn't want to say why and I felt my cheeks heat. Jed was my alibi and I was sure sleeping with the suspect wasn't allowed.

"She was with me," Jed said, not elaborating. He didn't even stall in responding. My heart leapt in my chest. "She couldn't have signed the contract."

"You're sure?" the director poked.

His eyes held mine. "*Very* sure."

I licked my lips. "This means someone else did. And it wasn't Macon."

16

JED

"WE'RE LOOKING for the wrong person," I said. With the cell still in my hand, I lifted North up and onto her feet. Then I stood. Paced the deck. "Shit, Amy, have we been looking at Macon by mistake? That it's been someone else entirely within the company?"

She made a funny sound. Something like a grunt, but a little more ladylike. A groan, but she was too high up the food chain to outwardly respond to a possible fuck up. It was frustration and eye-opening epiphany.

I turned to North, set my free hand on my hip. After I'd gotten out of bed, I'd pulled on my jeans, nothing else, thinking it would be easy to strip and move onto round two.

"You said you signed the land contract last night. Who knew?" I asked North. She'd only pulled on my t-shirt. Her hard nipples were hard to miss, poking at the letters on the front. She'd felt good in my lap, but it was fucking distracting.

She leaned against the rail and the dogs came up onto the porch. She patted them absently as she looked to me. "My assistant, Julian."

"Julian Zeman?" the director asked.

I moved to stand in front of North so the director could hear her.

"Yes," she confirmed. "I signed it, called him to notify him it was done and to ensure the bank wired the money."

"Why?" my boss asked.

She looked up at me. Her blue eyes held doubt and resolve.

"Why did I sign the contract?" she repeated.

"Yes."

Her head tipped to the side. Her long hair was tousled and I liked the sight of her. Mussed. In my t-shirt. Here. A warm breeze cut across the deck, and she tucked a lock behind her ear.

"I didn't know Jed was undercover. Then."

I gave her a nod to continue.

"I wasn't... convinced of his interest in me."

She'd doubted me. Even last night. *After.*

So much had changed since then. Had her lack of trust forced her to sign the contract which in turn made the director believe her guilty? She'd completed the deal with Marshall so she'd know I wasn't sniffing around solely to finish that job for him, which had been my original intention. Why hadn't she told me when she'd taken me to her bed?

Shit, all those answers. I'd pushed her into revealing everything about what Macon had done. Spanked her even. It had been my goal to get her out of her head. I'd done that, but one of the results was me being in the dark about the contract because I'd made her forget all about it.

"Interest in you? Jed, are you—"

"You've wanted to get answers from a Wainright for months," I snapped. "You've got one on the horn. Focus, Director."

"When you're back in the office, we need to have a talk," she replied, her voice laced with authority. Like I gave a fuck.

"I won't be back in the office," I told her. "I sent my two week notice to HR this morning."

North wasn't the only one signing papers. Her eyes

widened. Yeah, I'd surprised her right back. I had the ranch. I had this cabin. I had Jock and his family I needed to know better. I had North.

"Jed, think this through," the director said.

I tipped North's chin up so she couldn't look away. My gaze shifted between her eyes and mouth.

"I have." I spoke to my boss but studied North. The blueness of her eyes. The freckle on the side of her nose I hadn't seen before. "Don't worry, everyone around here thinks I'm a disgraced agent. Nothing you do now can make that worse."

She huffed. Then sighed. "Continue, Miss Wainright."

North swallowed, thought for a second, as if my announcement had made her forget the conversation. "I signed the Marshall contract after hours. Probably eight-thirty."

"How long has he—Julian—been your assistant?" she asked.

"Two years."

"He has access to all your files."

"Yes. He knows more about what I do than I do. All good assistants are that way."

"He had access to Macon?" she asked.

North considered. "Of course. I assume he talked mostly with Macon's assistant, Janice. Macon didn't have time for anyone he didn't deem important. Hell, he didn't even *see* them. You think Julian signed the logger contract for me?"

"If he worked for Macon on the side, then he could have signed contracts for you. Things you didn't know about. Like the land lease."

"I'd have known if the corporation bought land and leased it to loggers. It's not like that can slip by anyone. I mean, even if I didn't get wind, accounting would have. We might be a billion-dollar company, but paying millions for land is hard to hide."

"Unless someone in accounting's in on it too," the director added.

"I asked Julian for all of Macon's open contracts and I read through them yesterday," North continued. "That's how I learned about the deal with Marshall. Well, first from you," she said, looking at me and when I'd come to her office. "It was in the pile. There was nothing in there about a logging lease."

"Julian left it out intentionally then," I assumed.

"I'll go to the office and confront him."

North's words made me laugh. "Fuck no. Someone shot at you driving down the road. Until we know who's after you, you're staying here."

"Where's here?" the director asked.

"Somewhere safe," I countered, not telling her. I was on a burner phone even she couldn't trace.

"Jed, I want this done," North said, setting her hand on my chest. My bare chest. Which meant my dick went hard at the feel of her touching me. "If this stuff, and I mean the contracts, not the shooting, keeps happening, then Macon isn't really gone. I need him and his shit out of my life for good. You taught me that."

"I got you out here to keep you safe and you want me to turn around and put you in danger?"

She gave a little shrug. "I don't want to be shot at again. I might be stubborn, but I'm not stupid. But if Julian's behind all this, then I want to know."

I agreed with her, but I didn't like it.

"I'll confront Julian—"

"We," I butt in. "We'll confront him. You're not doing it alone." No fucking way.

She gave me a small smile. "We'll confront him and if it turns out we're wrong or he's not involved in the shooting, we'll come back here."

A squirrel ran across the porch rail. Boozer stirred, hopped up and chased after it. Eddie didn't even stir.

"Fine, but there are hundreds of people in your office building. I can't protect you there." I was losing my shit thinking about it.

"Then somewhere else remote. This is Montana," she countered.

"I won't have you driving around with a lunatic with a rifle out there."

She smiled at me, went up on her tiptoes and kissed my jaw. "Then it's a good thing I have a helicopter."

17

NORTH

IT TOOK A WHILE, because Jed was beyond stubborn. It felt good to have someone be protective, but he took the alpha male thing to the extreme. Then I remembered the way the windshield of my SUV shattered from a bullet and how I'd felt thinking I might die, and I gave in. We finally came up with a plan to confront Julian and for Jed not to have a coronary.

It might not have been Julian. Someone else could have electronically signed a contract for me. Hell, there was an entire Contracts Department. They made them so that meant they could sign them.

No one could get away with falsifying signatures

on known contracts. They'd be fired. But the one with the loggers seemed to be off the books. Julian hadn't even shared the paperwork for it, which meant one of two things. He didn't know about it and that was why he didn't include it in the stack he'd given me, or he knew about it and that was why he'd kept it from me.

That didn't explain the shooter or why someone wanted me dead. I couldn't sign a logger contract if I wasn't breathing. During our conversation with the FBI director, we couldn't even determine if the two issues went together.

All I knew was that I needed to clear my name. To get the FBI off my back. To bury Macon completely. I'd thought he'd been gone when I'd dropped a handful of dirt onto his coffin. I wasn't going to take the fall for whatever he'd been up to.

Unlike Jed, the director had been easy to convince. She wanted her case closed at all costs. I was just a person of interest to her. Nothing more. While I had to assume she didn't want me dead, she set the risks to my health and safety at different parameters than Jed.

Only when he'd felt the plan was solid—and he could stay in control of the situation—did he relent. With reinforcements. My brothers.

Whatever he'd talked about with South had swayed him. He trusted them. After we hung up with the director, we put the plan in motion, first connecting with South again and getting him and East and West in on it. I would summon Julian to the ranch the next day. While I might be a workaholic, even I would take the day off after someone tried to kill me.

So there was nothing to do except for Jed to strip me of his t-shirt and take me back to bed. Eat lasagna he'd pulled from the freezer. Play fetch with the dogs. Make me come—without me touching myself—until I passed out in his arms.

I trusted Jed. It seemed ridiculous, but I set the true proof of that onto the fact that I gave myself over to him. Let go completely. Knew he'd catch me if I fell. He brought me to orgasm.

Just as he'd planned since he'd laid eyes on me at the wake.

The next morning Paul landed the helicopter in the field in front of the cabin, the blades whipping the tops of the pines and sending some of the wildflowers into the air. Every bit of tension Jed had lost from our day of isolation and sex was back. I was in my dress and heels from the day before, at least until we were on the ranch and I could change. Jed had taken my panties and wouldn't give them back, so I was commando.

He had a gun tucked into the back of his jeans.

Now that I knew all of his truths, so much more made sense. His constant vigilance. His need for control. His protectiveness. If he had his way, I'd be handcuffed to the bed once again. Safe.

I loved being in bed with Jed, but I wanted to get to know him. If he liked crunchy or smooth peanut butter. Hell, if he was allergic to the stuff. I knew he was my man. Even after only a few days, I knew he was the guy for me. I wanted to be with him without any secrets. Without the past looming over us. I only wanted to look to the future. With him. However that would look.

If someone had told me my life would be like this a week ago, I'd have laughed. No way would I trust a man. Let one do the things Jed did. Tell me what to do. No, I'd have laughed not because of that, but because it made me hot.

And, of course, no way would I have even imagined Macon being dead. Maybe it was the one thing Macon did for me that was good.

Dying.

East hopped from the helicopter, bent at the waist to duck the low rotors, and came over to us. Jed tossed him his keys as East would drive Jed's truck with the dogs back to the ranch.

The thing everyone agreed on was that I wasn't

going anywhere by car.

No one could follow a helicopter from here in a vehicle, not in this terrain. Since the helicopter hadn't been at the house because of the weather yesterday morning, no one who might be watching the ranch would know it was even being used. No shooter would know where to sit and wait.

With the noise of the rotors, we didn't talk. East gave me a fierce hug, then pushed me toward Jed and the helicopter.

It took less than an hour and we were back at the ranch. I was safe inside and away from windows.

South and West were waiting. Before I went upstairs to change, I called Julian. My brothers and Jed were standing before me, listening. Hovering, as if Julian could cause me harm through the phone.

As usual, he answered on the first ring.

"I've been so worried. Everyone in the building's been talking about what happened," he said.

"I'm fine," I replied, glancing up at Jed. We were in the kitchen and he gripped the edge of the granite. I wouldn't mention to Julian how I'd been scared. I never shared anything but business with my assistant. "Look, obviously I'm not coming into the office."

"Right."

"I need Macon's files you pulled for me. They're on

my desk. Plus anything else that's come in, which I'm sure is plenty." Besides the few days after Macon died, I never took a day off. I was behind.

"It's all waiting for you. I rearranged your schedule." Just as I expected. He anticipated what I needed which was why he was a great assistant.

"In-person meetings will have to be video," I said. "For the next few days until the police investigate."

I had no idea what was going on with the police. I hadn't been questioned. I was sure South had given them a full accounting and they were working on it. But if Julian really was involved—

"Done," he said, efficient as usual.

"I can't review paperwork over video though," I added. "Bring them here, please."

While I wasn't belligerent to my employees, I would never *ask* Julian to come to the ranch. I told him what to do, with manners, and he did it.

"Be there in two hours."

"Thanks, Julian. I don't know what I would do without you." I didn't, actually. He was very good at his job. I didn't know if that meant he'd hid his misdeeds from me or if he was just going about his day as usual.

I hung up and I walked right to Jed, wrapped my arms around him. I loved that I could now seek comfort from him.

"If he's guilty, we'll know," Jed said, kissing the top of my head.

I looked to South and West, who nodded, crossed their arms over their broad chests.

For the first time, I realized, I wasn't alone.

18

JED

I'D BEEN with the FBI for almost twenty years. I'd seen everything. Handled the stress. Coped with danger. Been shot at. I'd dealt with it all without breaking a sweat.

But North saying my name in that scared voice the day before through the phone had taken years off my life.

For the first time ever, I had a liability. A weakness. I loved someone enough that if they were being harmed or threatened that it made me lose my shit.

I'd loved my parents. I was getting close with my

brother and his family again. I would not see harm come to them.

North Wainright though... she was my Achilles heel. My heart. A part of me. That was why I'd resigned from the FBI. I couldn't be away from her. The need to protect was too great. It would be impossible to go off on a mission now. I'd have to come to terms with letting her leave my sight, let alone this house. She was independent as fuck and smothering her wasn't going to work. Or handcuffing her to my bed. Although I did remember the perks of that, ones she'd enjoyed immensely.

Putting her in the same room with a man who might *possibly* be an attempted murderer and other things made me panic. I tried not to lose my shit. When South and West looked my way, they understood.

They'd underestimated North and what she was capable of. Of what she'd done for them. They wouldn't now. Neither would I. We'd worked on the plan. Ensured she was protected.

When Julian pulled up, South met him at the door and pointed him to us in Macon's office with all the fucking animal heads on the walls. Where this all began.

I'd met Julian briefly the other day in North's office. I pegged him at twenty-five and just under six feet. If he exercised, it was lifting a hair dryer. He was in dress pants, crisp white button-up shirt and tie. Like North when she was dressed for work, he would fit in better in a big city than Montana. He had more product in his dark hair that most women and I'd wager his nails were manicured. I didn't have great gaydar, but it was pretty obvious he batted for the other team. The one thing he wasn't doing was lusting after North.

His steps faltered when he saw me, but with North as his boss, he couldn't ruffle easily. Eddie followed him in, dropped on the floor at my feet.

North stood from behind the desk. The hard surface where I'd spread her wide and eaten her out. My dick got hard remembering, which was an inconvenience.

North was casually dressed in a pair of jeans and a black V-neck t-shirt. She'd showered and pulled her hair back into a low ponytail and had skipped makeup. I liked her this way, although she'd be wearing my FBI t-shirts around the house from now on.

Easy access.

He set the pile of papers he'd brought with him

down on the desk between them, kept a leather portfolio in his hand.

"Thanks," she said, giving him a small smile. "Sit. I'm sure you have a list."

He settled into the leather chair next to mine, glanced at me. Ignored Eddie who was already snoring.

"Oh, you remember Jed Barnett. He works for John Marshall. He stopped in to thank me for finalizing the land deal. The wire went through," she added. "Thanks for taking care of that."

"Of course," Julian said.

"Jed was wondering after the logging lease." North looked at him with an open expression. Expectant.

Julian was one cool dude. He paused for a second, if that. "What lease?"

North played it cool and shrugged her slim shoulders and looked to me. "Jed can explain it better since I didn't know about it until a few minutes ago."

Julian shifted his focus to me.

"Caston Logging," I said. "Macon was telling me about his arrangement. Before he died."

One—definitely waxed—brow went up on Julian's forehead. "He talked to you about it?"

I nodded. No question Julian knew how shady

Marshall was. Since he believed I worked for him, then I was too.

I set my forearms on the arm of the leather chair. Crossed my ankle over my knee. Tried to play it casual instead of holding a gun to his head to get him to talk. No judge was going to accept a coerced confession. I couldn't allow him to walk free because of something I did. "It's in play now that she finalized the land purchase."

Julian's eyes ping ponged between us.

"You know we're... a thing," North said. Her blush wasn't a lie. "I mean, you had to have heard us at the wake."

Julian flipped open the portfolio to the pristine notepad within. "It's not my place to comment."

"And that's why you're so good at your job. Your discretion," she added.

He preened at that. I wasn't happy that he'd overheard me getting North get off, although I hadn't cared who'd heard at the time. While the house had been emptied of guests, there'd been caterers in the kitchen and other people working the wake. I had to assume even a funeral director since there had been a casket in the foyer. Obviously, Julian had been somewhere in this monstrosity during the event.

"We've been together for over a month," North said.

Julian frowned, as if having this get past him wasn't something he'd considered.

"I kept my standing appointment with the... agency, but met Jed instead."

The fucking escort. There went my hard on, because it was literally a *fucking escort* she'd seen for a long time.

Before me. The asshole might have filled a need, but he'd never quenched a thirst or made her whole.

North waved her hand. "We have much to go over, so I'll stay focused. Jed told me about the logging deal. I held off on Marshall signing his contract as long as I could." She leaned forward, set her forearms on the desk. "You couldn't expect me to just sign right away after the funeral. I had to let the man sweat. Let him know that Mason might be dead, but a Wainright still holds the power."

"Smart," Julian added.

"Now, that lease. I didn't see the paperwork for it in the files you shared yesterday. Is it in here?" she asked, not looking at Julian as she pulled the stack toward her across the desk.

This was the moment. Proof of his inclusion. Or not.

"It's not in there," he admitted. "I signed it for you yesterday."

She looked up at him, feigning surprise. "Oh?"

He squirmed. "I didn't... we didn't. I mean, Macon didn't want you to know."

North gave a little shrug. "Not surprising. He's dead. I know now. The question is, how do *you* know about it?"

"Well, Macon."

"I thought you were my assistant. Or were you working for him?" She tilted her head.

He shrugged but looked at his lap. "Like you said, he's dead. I work for you."

"Then why did you have someone shoot at North?" I asked.

We were going to be here all day. North could handle a roomful of suits. Negotiate a million-dollar contract, but she had no fucking clue how to interrogate a witness.

I stood, leaned against the desk. North was behind me, although I didn't block her view of Julian entirely. As I crossed my arms over my chest, I watched his every nuance.

Eddie woke up. He lifted his head and looked up at me.

"I don't know what you're talking about," Julian said.

"You might have been North's assistant, but what else did you do for Macon? How many other deals did you hide from her?"

His Adam's apple bobbed as he swallowed hard.

"Is Janice aware of what's going on?" North asked.

He laughed. "Janice? She couldn't empty a bucket if the instructions were on the bottom."

"Macon didn't hire idiots." I thought for a moment. "Or maybe he did. She was a front, wasn't she? A woman at a desk answering phones and getting coffee."

As he straightened his tie with the manicured fingers, it all became clear.

"You were in love with him," I guessed, but stated as fact.

Behind me, North popped to her feet. "What?"

Julian stood as well, suddenly very, very nervous.

"What did Macon promise you?" I added.

"I don't know what you're talking about," he snapped.

"North, who told you that Macon had been with his mistress when he died?" I asked but didn't turn to look at her.

"The police," she replied.

"He was with you, wasn't he, Julian? He died while you were together in bed. You called someone... ah, you called the escort service North used and had a woman show up. You paid her to call the police. To pretend he'd died while fucking her, not you."

North sucked in a breath, obviously putting it together.

"Macon Wainright wasn't into women, was he?" I pushed. "He was having sex with you. Telling you things. Got you to believe you meant something to him when you weren't anything more than a pawn."

After what North shared, it was plausible. She wasn't the only one he'd used.

"I wasn't a pawn!" Julian said, eyes narrowed in anger. "He loved me. I did things for him. Got deals signed. Pushed things past the ice princess. I told him I could do it and I proved it."

Fuck. Me. I'd been right.

Eddie sat up, leaned against my leg.

"Why did you try to have me killed?" North asked. Her voice wasn't sharp or angry. It was sad. She recognized how Julian had been used. The difference between North and Julian was that she'd never given in to Macon. Never believed his lies. She'd stood up to him.

Julian hadn't been so strong.

"Caston paid me to take care of it. You see, I solve everyone's problems."

"The owner of the logging company paid you to kill North and sign the contract for her."

I had to clearly outline his guilt. Aloud.

He nodded. "Yes."

"She didn't die," I said. I wanted to grab him and rip his head off, but I needed his full admission.

Julian flicked his gaze to North. "I know."

Julian pulled a gun from beneath his portfolio. I knew he had to be carrying some kind of weapon. To finish off the job that had been botched. *If* he'd been involved.

He was. He was at the center of it. The organizer. He was a guy who'd fallen for the biggest bullshitter of them all.

My blood went cold at the sight. This moment was why I'd been adamant North stay cuffed to the bed.

I slid over in front of North, blocking her. The room was big, but the chairs were close to the desk. I was easily able to reach out and shove the weapon to the side but didn't get to it before Eddie snarled and lunged, biting Julian's leg. He howled in pain, the gun swinging wide. He fired, blowing a hole in the wall.

South, West, and East stormed into the room, weapons up.

"Eddie, down!" North yelled and the dog let go.

I tackled Julian to the ground and grabbed the gun. Knelt on his back and yanked his wrists behind his back. I slipped cuffs from my back pocket and put them on him as I ducked my head and peeked under the desk. There was North, big eyed, watching.

Eddie crawled toward me, tail thumping, then licked my neck.

I laughed at Eddie's surprise burst of energy and affection as I gave her a wink.

South hauled Julian up.

"He hated you!" Julian shouted, his cool veneer cracking. "All of you."

The local police had been outside—the patrol SUV tucked into a garage stall out of sight—in case we needed them. They stormed through the door as they must've heard the shot. Two in uniform stood in the open doorway. They knew I was FBI and what was going down and were waiting for instructions from me.

I went around the desk as North stood, wrapped her in my arms.

"Yeah, fucker. We knew that already," South said.

His jaw was clenched, and I'd never seen him so pissed. I didn't blame him.

"You don't know why. Why he hated all of you," Julian spat. His groomed hair was messy, locks falling every which way. His face was red, eyes narrowed and full of anger.

"Because we're not his kids," North answered, her cheek pressed against my chest.

19

NORTH

THE POLICE TOOK JULIAN AWAY. The FBI was arresting the head of Caston Logging. Jed's boss had been debriefed. I was officially cleared.

Jed was officially unemployed.

He didn't seem to mind.

Finally, we were all on the patio that overlooked the pool. Not to be mistaken for the patio off the dining room or the patio off of the great room. South, East, and West were sprawled out in comfortable wrought iron chairs with thick cushions. East's feet were on a low coffee table. South had a beer in his hand. West had reheated the uneaten chicken enchiladas and we'd plowed through them as we should have the other night.

I was on a lounger tucked against Jed's chest. His Stetson was on the small table next to us. The sun had dipped behind the house and there was a gentle breeze. All was quiet and for once in my life... peaceful.

Jed hadn't stopped touching me since Julian had pulled out his gun, and I was fine with that. It seemed I wanted the contact just as much. Needed it.

Eddie and Boozer were sleeping at our feet. Eddie was snoring, and if the scent I caught was right, Boozer had farted. Eddie's little spurt of fierceness earlier had surprised us all and we'd be giving him extra treats for a while

"I still can't believe it," West said, staring out at the million—no *billion*—dollar view. I wasn't sure if he saw it or was processing everything in his head.

"Macon was gay," South said, as if verbalizing it was the only way to work through it. "I never saw that one coming."

"We're not his kids," East added. "I'd hoped that was true growing up, but fuck... it was true."

"We'll find out for sure," I said. We had to know one way or the other. "Do DNA testing. Shit, I had Mrs. Sanchez get rid of all his things." I tipped my chin up, looked to Jed, panicked a little. Had my need to rid myself of Macon kept us from ever learning the truth?

"One of his cars has got to have his DNA in it," Jed guessed and I relaxed.

"He was a slob," I told him. "The cleaners picked up after him at the house, but he didn't let anyone touch his cars. You're right. There has to be cigar stubs and those stupid mint toothpicks he used."

West gave a huff which I took as a sign he knew what I was talking about.

"You think that's why he hated us so much? Because we weren't really his?" East asked. "I mean, it explains why a father could plan to have his kid's leg broken. Since I wasn't his kid and all. Fuck, he hated us."

It made sense. Macon's hatred had been deep. I never understood why he'd never liked any of his kids. Why we were such... burdens to him. Now it made sense. We were reminders of his wife's infidelity, although I had no doubt he'd been unfaithful in return. I had to wonder if our mother was a front for his alternative lifestyle. So many questions.

"Then who is our father?" South asked as if sensing exactly what I wanted to know as well.

"Or fathers," West argued. "It's not like we look

alike. Obviously East and I have the same one. Duh. I'm not saying Mom was a slut or something, but she had to know about dad."

I'd been five when she'd died. I barely remembered her and I knew East and West didn't at all.

"I'd like to think she found love with someone," I said almost wistfully. Now that I'd met Jed, knew what it felt like to be wanted, and want in return, I hoped she'd had it too.

Jed kissed the top of my head. "Want to get out of here?"

I shifted, looked up at him. His dark eyes that saw everything were looking between mine, dipping to my mouth.

"Yeah." I wanted to be alone with Jed more than anything. We had no answers now. My brothers were going to sit and think. Maybe shout some more things.

He helped me to my feet and I looked to South, West, and East. "We're going to get out of here."

South stood. Nodded. "Good. Work can wait a week or two."

"A week or two? I meant tonight," I countered.

He shook his head. "No. Go. We don't want to see you for at least a week." He held up his hand. "Before you say anything about work, the company's not going to go under."

Jed wrapped an arm around my waist and kissed the top of my head. "A week."

I was going to argue, out of habit, for a second. But really, I didn't want to. A week with Jed alone? Yes, please.

South held out his hand to Jed. They shook. "Take care of our sister."

"You know I will."

I gave a little wave to East and West who were smiling. They liked Jed. They liked me with Jed.

Things had changed. We were different now. Secrets revealed. The past couldn't hurt us any longer. We were stronger. A team.

Jed led me inside. "Where do you want to go?" he asked as we cut through the great room.

There was no delay in my answer. "Your cabin. Definitely."

I loved it there.

"I'm selfish. I want you all to myself," I admitted, tugging him to stop, then hooking my hand behind his neck.

His eyes gleamed and he kissed me, as if he couldn't help himself.

When I lifted my head, I debated dragging him to my room and my bed, which was much closer than the cabin. "Let me pack a bag," I murmured.

"Won't need it, princess."

"To stay for at least a week I need—"

He set a finger over my lips. "You need my t-shirt and nothing else. You know what's going to happen to your panties if you bring them."

"You're going to take them, then fuck me," I said, my voice breathy with anticipation.

He growled. "When I walked into Macon's wake, all I thought about was that I didn't fuck on command. Because that was what Marshall wanted."

I stiffened at his admission, but I waited. He had more to say and the one thing he wanted me to do was to trust him. I did.

"I'd been completely wrong," he said. "I do fuck on command."

My mouth dropped open and I stared at him, confused. "If there's one guy who doesn't like to be bossed around, it's you."

He shrugged and the corner of his mouth tipped up. "What changed, princess, is who is bossing me around."

Oh. He was talking about me.

"I thought... I thought you were in charge."

His smile widened then and he kissed me once more. "That's right. I'm in charge. But you're the one who holds all the power."

"Really?"

He nodded.

"You rule me, princess."

God, that was hot. "Then fuck me," I breathed.

He tossed me over his shoulder and carried me from the house, Boozer and Eddie following. I assumed we were headed to his truck and the cabin, but I didn't care where we were headed.

As long as I was with Jed.

The secret is out! Ready for more Billionaire Ranch? Continue on with South!

IT WAS her ass I saw first. Perfect. Lush like a peach. Wiggling as it stuck out of the fridge. I paused and stared because... I wasn't dead. I leaned against the mudroom doorway, crossed my arms and enjoyed the view. After a morning fighting with a piece of metal that wouldn't bend the way I wanted, this was a treat.

She was a treat. I hadn't seen the rest of her besides the way her jeans were molded, but so far, so good.

Hell, so far, incredible.

I'd hated this house for years, just now finally getting comfortable inside these walls that had seen too much when I was a kid. The view of a perfect ass was better. So much better.

One twitch of that perfection and I'm rock-hard. Like one stroke and I'd come kind of hard. A teenager who couldn't control his dick kind of hard.

She tugged out a glass shelf and set it in the sink filled with soapy water. Food items like mustard and milk were on the counter. Then she saw me. Gasped. She yanked the earbuds free and let them dangle by the cord.

Fuck, the rest of her… my dick swelled and spurted pre-cum. *Just like that.*

"God, you scared me," she panted, then offered me a shaky smile. One that said I'm not sure if I'm safe with you.

That voice. Soft, deep. Breathy. I imagined what it would sound like saying my name. *South. Yes, South! More.*

"Shit, you're beautiful," I told her, shifting in the hope my zipper wouldn't leave a permanent mark on my dick.

She really was beautiful. Maybe it was the artist in me that noticed, because she sure as hell was trying to hide it. Dark hair pulled back in a sloppy bun that hid its length. I could tell it would fall to at least the center of her back by the thickness. Slide over pink nipples. Glasses hid her wide eyes, but I couldn't miss the chocolate color. No, aged whiskey. Deep and rich. She wore no makeup, but she didn't need it, especially the way a deep blush colored her cheeks.

I wanted to tug on that hair tie and let those thick locks cascade over her shoulders. Kiss those full lips. Yank off that loose t-shirt and see every inch she hid beneath. Not all that well because those hips were wide, that rack full and more than a handful. I'd surprised her and I was an ass for not apologizing—and for thinking so long with my dick.

"Beautiful?" She rolled her eyes. "I'm up to my arms in soap suds and smell like furniture polish. You get kicked by a horse or something?"

It seemed like it, looking at her. I'd never felt like this before. Never had a reaction so strongly. Oh, I'd had my fair share of women, but they'd fulfilled a need. Nothing more.

This? This was way fucking more than need. It was like something in me shifted. That I'd been waiting for this moment. For her.

She was young. Legal, definitely, but I had to wonder if she could buy herself a drink. No wonder I didn't know her. A small town meant knowing everyone and their business, but she'd probably been in elementary school when I went off to college. That meant I'd been waiting for her to be old enough to be mine. That was if she'd even grown up here.

Who was she?

I was going to find out. I was at the big house to see Jed. He would know. Since he got together with North, he knew everything that went on around here.

As I took a step closer, she held up her hand. "Stop right there."

I froze, then couldn't help but smile at this pint-sized woman bossing me around. In my sister's house. Hell, Jed could wait.

"What?" I asked. "I won't hurt you."

I needed her to know I might be a foot taller and probably a hundred pounds heavier, but I'd never do anything to harm her.

"Don't bring all that dirt in here," she said, looking me over. "You might be a hot cowboy, but you're going to make a mess."

I grinned. "*Hot cowboy*, huh?"

She rolled her eyes again, then pointed at me. "You don't need that fact pointed out. The dirt though…"

I took off my Stetson and looked down at myself. My white t-shirt had dirt stains, a small tear where I'd snagged the fabric on a sharp corner of my latest work. Metal was unforgiving and messy. My jeans had seen better days, the knees soiled from where I'd knelt on the floor of my studio to weld a section in place. My boots were dusty and worn. Clearly, I didn't look like one of the homeowners. While North was the only one who lived here now, I'd grown up in this mansion until I went off to college. She'd remained, stuck here with Macon, our father.

No, from what North's ex-assistant Julian had said, he wasn't our fucking father after all.

It didn't matter. This was Wainright Ranch and I was a Wainright. I belonged here.

Obviously, she didn't know that. I didn't know who she was, but reading the white script on the t-shirt over her perfect right tit, she worked for Nancy's Cleaning Service. She was one of the maids? If her last name wasn't Wainright, she worked here.

I might have been a billionaire, but I respected anyone who earned their living the hard way. Through hard work. Unlike Macon, who'd married it. He might've earned a hefty salary as CEO of Wainright Holdings, but the real cash had been our mother's.

"I'm a little dirty, huh?" I said, chagrined. As a sculptor, I never stayed clean on a project.

"Don't tell me North gets mad at you if there's a mess. Or a messy person interrupting you."

"North?" she asked, pushing her glasses up.

"Mad?" She looked surprised. "She's a sweetheart."

I opened my mouth to argue. My sister? The ice princess? At least *former* ice princess since her man Jed had thawed her? Since most of her stress died with Macon?

"Don't say anything otherwise," she added, giving me a stern librarian look through those glasses.

I frowned. "You afraid of being fired?" That wasn't going to happen. Although if I had my way, she wouldn't be working here long. I didn't know her dreams. Her plans. I doubted they were scrubbing someone else's fridge. I'd help her with them. See them come true.

"No. Her father passed away recently, and she's been through a lot. The entire family has. Just because they have money doesn't mean they don't have hardship."

I blinked. "You're right," I agreed, knowing the truth of her words firsthand. I only wasn't expecting her to say so.

She was defending North. And me. She didn't even know it. I liked her even more. I was used to women flinging themselves at me. At my money. I didn't look like a million bucks all the time like North. More like a *billion*. This place wasn't nicknamed Billionaire Ranch for nothing.

I lived in a simple farmhouse down the road, refusing to live in this place. Worked with my hands sculpting metal from scrap to art. Lived off my commissions, never touching a dime of my trust. Sure, I ate the Wainright cook's food when I came over. I enjoyed the liquor cabinet from time to time. I rode the horses. On occasion, I even flew in the helicopter that was North's main commute to the office.

But I never wanted to be known for being South Wainright, billionaire.

I was just a man.

And I'd found my woman.

She didn't know it yet.

Continue on with South!

BONUS CONTENT

Guess what? I've got some bonus content for you! Sign up for my mailing list. There will be special bonus content for some of my books, just for my subscribers. Signing up will let you hear about my next release as soon as it is out, too (and you get a free book...wow!)

As always...thanks for loving my books and the wild ride!

Vanessa

JOIN THE WAGON TRAIN!

If you're on Facebook, please join my closed group, the Wagon Train! Don't miss out on the giveaways and hot cowboys!

https://www.facebook.com/groups/vanessavalewagontrain/

GET A FREE BOOK!

Join my mailing list to be the first to know of new releases, free books, special prices and other author giveaways.

http://freeromanceread.com

ALSO BY VANESSA VALE

For the most up-to-date listing of my books:

vanessavalebooks.com

On A Manhunt

Man Hunt

Man Candy

Man Cave

Man Splain

Man Scape

Man Handle

Man Spread

The Billion Heirs

Scarred

Flawed

Broken

Alpha Mountain

Hero

Rebel

Warrior

Billionaire Ranch

North

South

East

West

Bachelor Auction

Teach Me The Ropes

Hand Me The Reins

Back In The Saddle

Wolf Ranch

Rough

Wild

Feral

Savage

Fierce

Ruthless

Two Marks

Untamed

Tempted

Desired

Enticed

More Than A Cowboy

Strong & Steady

Rough & Ready

Wild Mountain Men

Mountain Darkness

Mountain Delights

Mountain Desire

Mountain Danger

Grade-A Beefcakes

Sir Loin of Beef

T-Bone

Tri-Tip

Porterhouse

Skirt Steak

Small Town Romance

Montana Fire

Montana Ice

Montana Heat

Montana Wild

Montana Mine

Steele Ranch

Spurred

Wrangled

Tangled

Hitched

Lassoed

Bridgewater County

Ride Me Dirty

Claim Me Hard

Take Me Fast

Hold Me Close

Make Me Yours

Kiss Me Crazy

Mail Order Bride of Slate Springs

A Wanton Woman

A Wild Woman

A Wicked Woman

Bridgewater Ménage

Their Runaway Bride

Their Kidnapped Bride

Their Wayward Bride

Their Captivated Bride

Their Treasured Bride

Their Christmas Bride

Their Reluctant Bride

Their Stolen Bride

Their Brazen Bride

Their Rebellious Bride

Their Reckless Bride

Bridgewater Brides World

Lenox Ranch Cowboys

Cowboys & Kisses

Spurs & Satin

Reins & Ribbons

Brands & Bows

Lassos & Lace

Montana Men

The Lawman

The Cowboy

The Outlaw

Standalones

Relentless

All Mine & Mine To Take

Bride Pact

Rough Love

Twice As Delicious

Flirting With The Law

Mistletoe Marriage

Man Candy - A Coloring Book

ABOUT VANESSA VALE

A USA Today bestseller, Vanessa Vale writes tempting romance with unapologetic bad boys who don't just fall in love, they fall hard. Her books have sold over one million copies. She lives in the American West where she's always finding inspiration for her next story.

vanessavaleauthor.com

facebook.com/vanessavaleauthor
instagram.com/vanessa_vale_author
amazon.com/author/vanessavale
bookbub.com/profile/vanessa-vale
tiktok.com/@vanessavaleauthor

Printed in Dunstable, United Kingdom

67907299R00147